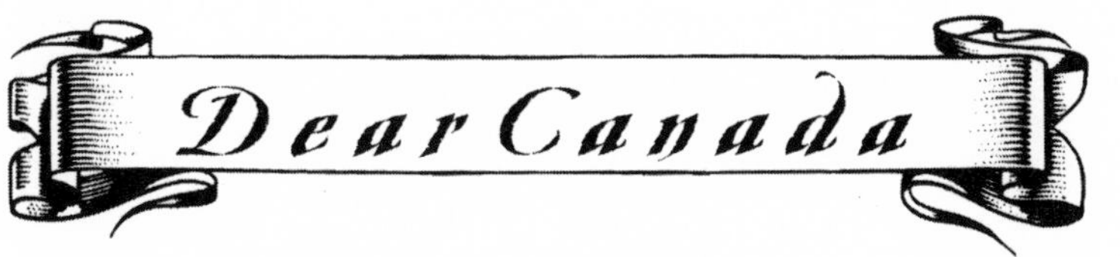

Blood Upon Our Land

The North West Resistance Diary of Josephine Bouvier

BY MAXINE TROTTIER

Scholastic Canada Ltd.

Batoche,
District of Saskatchewan,
1885

Le 31 décembre 1884

Before he went back to his cabin tonight, Moushoom gave me this diary. It is as colourful as Mama's most beautiful *saencheur flechee,* the one I will wear over my shoulder at tomorrow night's party. He is so dear, my grandfather. He said that if Mama were here she would have given me a diary much like this one. I think he is correct, since Mama was the one who taught me to read and write, after all. "Your mother kept a diary herself," Moushoom reminded me. He was certain it contained many interesting stories.

Then he insisted that I must pass on my stories in these pages, since if stories were not told, they would surely disappear. "And if the stories do disappear," he said, "so might our language and Métis way of life, for all are connected."

When I protested that I was not a storyteller as he is, and that I had no idea what I should write, Moushoom only laughed. "Write it all," he told me, "but it must be the truth, always the truth." I smiled when he said that I was not to worry. He will help me if I have no ideas.

Vers minuit

In a few minutes, a new year will be upon us. It will find we Bouviers as well and as happy as can be, although Mama's passing still saddens us. Even after almost two years, I still miss her so.

Earlier, Moushoom blessed our family as he does each year on this night, reminding us to keep our faith, our customs and our Michif language safe. In that way we would be true to our ancestors.

There. Papa has just fired his rifle, a shot to the west out the back door to see the old year out. And again, a shot to the east out the front door to welcome in this new year.

What will happen here in the months to come? There will be changes. Always there are changes, although I find I do not care for them much these days. Familiar things seem best. Nothing of much importance will ever take place here though, I suppose. Batoche is such a quiet place.

Le 1 janvier 1885

My day began with a good deal of cheerful fuss. "Not a book for her to write in," Adrian shouted when he saw this diary, insisting that all I would do now would be to write, write, write. Armand wondered how Moushoom could have done such a thing. (Armand is probably worried about who will cook his breakfast after Mass. He thinks too much about his belly.) I do not believe he even knew what he was asking, though. He is just a little boy who likes to copy his older brother. With both of them shouting there was quite a noise, but then that is often the case at our house. It is still a noisy happy home, in spite of our loss. Mama would be pleased about that.

The boys' words were nothing but nonsense, since I had already started the *galet,* the same way I do each morning, mixing the flour, lard, water and baking powder so that the balls of dough are ready to go onto the griddle later. It is Mama's recipe, but I will not try to write it down. She always said that, like common sense, making *galet* is one of those things you carry in your head.

Back to the fuss. Moushoom picked up the diary and shook it at them, saying they were rascals, that no other man in Batoche had such an educated granddaughter, one who had been reading almost since birth!

Here I must write that my grandfather sometimes pulls at facts until they are long and stretched. True, I *have* been reading and writing words since I was quite young, but not almost from the day I was born — almost thirteen years ago now. Papa sighed and shook his head, playing along with the boys. It was only the usual silliness and teasing, but I have to wonder what a stranger would think of us.

Besides, my brothers are proud of me, especially Adrian — perhaps because he is older and understands the importance of learning. I heard him saying so while I dressed for the party this evening. He went on about how wonderful it was that his sister could even read a newspaper to Moushoom when we are lucky enough to get one. Adrian also bragged to Papa and Moushoom how few young girls here could write and read so skillfully, and how I barely struggled with the printed English words. It was hard for me just then not to become puffed up with pride like a toad that has eaten too many crickets, but modesty is important.

Adrian did not say any of this to my face, of course. But if I am very quiet, and I can be *very* quiet, I can hear perfectly from my bedroom above the kitchen. That is because Mama insisted that Papa cut a hole in the floor so that the warmth from the stove would rise to me. Voices rise as well. *Mársee,* Mama!

Très tard

It was a wonderful *Zhour di Lāh* celebration, one that I will describe exactly, so that when I read it months from now, it will bring the evening back to me. And the next time I am able to meet with

Emma, we will remind each other of what a fine evening we had. Emma. It would be so much easier for us to talk together if she spoke Michif, and I had less trouble saying the English words correctly. We manage well enough in French, though.

Emma said that it was as fine as any party she could ever remember back in Toronto, where her parents' families still live. Perhaps she exaggerated a little, since they say that Toronto is a very grand place. In the English way, of course. On the other hand, Moushoom has told me that he once saw some English North-West Mounted Police having a party at Fort Carlton. The police drank tea. It must have been a very quiet party.

This one was not quiet. I could hear the sound of the fiddle music coming from Henri Baptiste Boyer's house even before we left in our sleigh, and it made me feel so light and so very happy. The air was still and cold, yet it carried the smells of the food that I, like others, had been preparing for days. I decided not to remind my brothers of my part in this once they began to gorge themselves. How saintly I felt at that moment, and how splendid, for under my good rabbit-skin coat I wore the new dress I made for myself last month. Mama's silver pocket watch hung around my neck on a red ribbon, and her sash lay over my shoulder.

Papa had brought his fiddle and as soon as we

went into the house, people began to call out to him, "Vylōōn! Vylōōn! Play for us!" Almost no one here calls him Michel. Instead, he is known as Vylōōn because he plays the fiddle so well. Papa joined the other players. He began with a tune called "Whiskey Before Breakfast," Moushoom's favourite. Tonight I believe Papa played that tune more wonderfully than ever.

Emma I spied at once, since with her blond hair and cheerful laugh she is easy to find in any crowd. As are her parents — I think they are as fair as she is. Emma took me aside and whispered that she hoped my brother would ask her to dance. This did not surprise me at all, since Adrian is a very handsome young man, with his green eyes so much like Papa's. I know she admires him, and I am certain that Adrian likes her very much, although I would not say so to either of them. I could not help myself, though, and I asked Emma if she knew that we Métis call the first day in *janvier* Kissing Day, since we greet each other with handshakes and kisses. How she blushed. I can tease as well as my brothers when I decide to.

Adrian danced once with me as Papa played the "Big John MacNeil Hornpipe," which is one of my favourite tunes. Then he danced many times with Emma. She and my brother make a fine couple, Adrian with his dark hair and brown skin and

Emma as sunny as a flower, even though she stumbled through the Red River jigs. Emma says people do not dance the Red River jig back in Ontario. Poor things, is what I say about those people. I also danced many times, but with no one in particular unless you count Edmond Swift Fox. We are *not* a couple. As for Moushoom, he sat with his old friend Joseph Ouellette and called out encouragement to the young dancers.

I am sure I counted more than a hundred people in Monsieur Boyer's house, and I vow that I could feel friendship in the air. Père André and Père Moulin stood together, no doubt discussing the state of our souls. There were babies in their mothers' arms, old men and women, and all the ages in between, eating and talking and dancing. All of my aunts and uncles and cousins were there — too many to list here, for we are a large family. I saw our neighbours the Ouellettes, the Fishers, the Dumonts, the young widow Pepin, the Letendres and others. People came from miles away.

The Riel family was there, of course. Like many men, Monsieur Riel wore a fine sash around his waist, one woven using many colours of wool. Near him stood William Jackson, who lives with them in a cabin on Moïse Ouellette's farm. The Riels' children ran about happily with the other young ones, Jean-Louis leading the way with little Marie-

Angelique behind him, while their mama and Monsieur Riel's cousin Monsieur Nolin watched. As for Louis Riel, he was the hero of the evening!

He was given a gift of money presented to him in an octopus bag, its four pairs of dangling legs all beautifully embroidered. Then a letter for Monsieur Riel from the settlement of St. Louis was read aloud. All I could hear was that the people did not want to let the New Year go by without expressing their respect and gratitude to him, because Armand was whining to be taken outside. He had eaten too many *bengs.* As usual. He should know by now that so much fried bread does not agree with him, but he cannot seem to resist the sweetness of it. He was sure he was going to be sick on the floor and shame himself, so I offered to take him home. Papa and the others could then enjoy the rest of the evening. Monsieur Riel was toasting all the Métis women in the room as I helped Armand into his *capot.* Then, just as we walked out the door, I heard Emma's parents join in as some people toasted Queen Victoria.

Moushoom says he saw a picture of Queen Victoria once, and she did not look as though she would enjoy much of anything. Still, I have to wonder what she would have thought of our party.

Le 2 janvier 1885

Mild weather. Madame Laframboise, a widow Papa probably danced with at the Boyers' home last night, came by this morning. She had brought us a *tart de vyawnd* made from venison and a bit of pork. I knew it would be only a bit of pork, since it is hard to come by this winter. Papa and our men were hunting, so I accepted the pie graciously.

It reminded me of the days just after Mama's passing, and the kindness of our neighbours and relatives. Madame Laframboise sometimes brings food to the house the way she did then, even though everyone knows I now prepare the meals for our family. My mother instructed me well. And Madame is not alone in bringing food either, as there are other widows keen to show Papa what fine cooks they are. *Abain,* they are like a flock of hens all chasing after the same rooster. I will try not to think about them. Besides, my *tart de vyawnd* is much tastier.

Le 3 janvier 1885

I would not bother to write that Edmond Swift Fox accompanied me

I should scratch that out. He accompanied *us* home the other night. I would never write it had the fact not caused such a fuss with Armand. How my little brother carried on about us being more than just friends! *Nichimoose, nichimoose,* he boldly chanted, though Edmond is not my sweetheart! It is hard to say who had the redder face, Edmond or me. Moushoom, though, laughed until he cried and even Papa joked about it a little. Still, it was all in good fun until Adrian, who sometimes sees humour in very little, I fear, said to Papa that he of all men should not make jokes about such a serious undertaking as marriage. Sometimes Adrian is impossible to understand.

Plus tard

I have been thinking about Edmond tonight, which I suppose is no surprise after the tormenting we both suffered. I have also been thinking about Emma. When she and her family first came here, she thought that Edmond was one of my brothers. I explained how he came to live with us, and how he came to have his name. That was when she told me about a place in Toronto called the orphanage. I believe that is the word, and to me it is a sad and ugly one. It is not the way of Métis people to send away children to live with strangers.

I remember that tears rose to Emma's eyes when I told her how Edmond's father had been caught in a blizzard and had frozen to death. When that happened, Edmond — he was called Edmond Sauvé, then, I explained — Edmond and his mother returned to her family at the One Arrow Reserve. I think the returning must have been a great comfort to them both.

I cannot actually recall when all of Edmond's family except him died of fevers one terrible winter. It was Mama who told me, and it brought tears to my eyes as it did to Emma's. I have lost my own mother, but even today, I cannot imagine losing *everyone.*

It makes sense that Edmond lives with Moushoom. After all, Moushoom was like a brother to Edmond's grandfather, back in the days when Gabriel Dumont led the big buffalo hunts. No orphanage for Edmond! Moushoom says that Edmond is excellent company and not nearly as noisy as certain people in the big house. I suppose that is why they prefer Moushoom's cabin near the river at the end of our farm. It is so quiet there, what with the trees that shelter it.

Mama loved Edmond, and I know he loved her in turn. It was she, after all, who insisted he come to us. Edmond visits her grave sometimes — I have seen him doing this — although he says nothing about the visiting. Yes, Edmond is a good friend.

Le 4 janvier 1885

It remains bitterly cold and the river is frozen over. That means people are able to cross the South Saskatchewan in sleighs. This is good, since neither the ferry that Monsieur Letendre has here, or the one down the way at Gabriel's Crossing, are running these days. Even though Monsieur Dumont no longer owns the ferry, the crossing is still named after him. Moushoom says that good names stick like pine gum to birchbark.

The *Northcote* is unable to carry goods up and down the river now, of course, though it brought all the poles and wire for the telegraph at Clarke's Crossing last fall. It is exciting to have a telegraph office fairly close to us. So many modern changes happening!

I have not heard the *Northcote's* whistle since that time, but I do hear Marie-Antoinette sing each Sunday. I have often thought I should write about her singing, since the words sound so amusing. And there. Now I have. Marie-Antoinette is not a woman, of course, but a bell, our beautiful silver-plated bell that hangs in the tower of St. Antoine de Padoue church here at Batoche. The day that Bishop Grandin baptized her, on *le 2 septembre,* giving Marie-Antoinette her name, was so exciting! It was such an important event that Père Fourmond, Père André, Père Touze and other priests came as guests. I felt very proud for Batoche that day.

Plus tard

Marie-Antoinette has made me remember something else. The date and the bishop's name — *Vital-Justin Grandin, Eveque de St. Albert* — are engraved upon the bell. A shield is also engraved there. Père Moulin says that the shield is the bishop's coat of arms, and that the images on it, a cross and a bent reed, mean that the bishop yields to the will of God. If that is so, then I have to say that I envy the bishop a little. Yielding to God's will is very hard for me at times.

Moushoom says that if the Bouviers had such a shield, there would have to be a buffalo on it. Armand thinks it should have a *beng.* Papa, though, has said that the Bouviers need nothing to show what we are. Our family's actions and honour are enough.

As for Marie-Antoinette, Père Moulin has told us that she was once a queen of France. I wonder if she was as well liked as Queen Victoria.

Le 5 janvier 1885

As has been planned, we are going to have a *bal à l'huile*. If someone read this diary, it would sound as though all we do is make merry, but a *bal à l'huile* means a great deal of work. Since the dance is held by lamplight, all the lamps — I have borrowed a number from Madame Letendre and Madame Pepin — had to be polished, the wicks trimmed and the lamps filled with oil.

Then there was the floor to sweep, the furniture to be moved out of the way for dancing, barn cats to shoo out. The cats do like to sleep under the stove. I washed and polished the glass in the windows, glass that Papa bought for Mama to replace the parchment they used at first. Some houses here still have parchment windows. I can remember Mama saying that the skin of a young deer lets in a good deal of light if it is properly scraped and stretched. She enjoyed her window glass more, though, poor Mama. But I must not dwell on that.

Moushoom helped with the cleaning, brushing the floorboards with the wing of a Canada goose. He took both the braided rugs and the hooked rugs outside to beat any dust out of them. He wound the clock, and then he put fresh cedar twigs in all the corners as well as over the windows and doors, for protection against evil. Some would say it is a strange thing that a man, such an old old man, would work inside the home, but Moushoom lived all those years alone after the last of his wives died. Of all the men in this house, he is the tidiest.

Baking, dusting. To work, Josephine! Make the house sparkle just as Mama would have.

Le 6 janvier 1885

Zhour de Rwāy

How I prayed at Mass on this holy feast day of the Three Kings. One decade of my rosary for patience, one decade for understanding, three for peace of mind. Moushoom, who still does not attend Mass — I had hoped that the new year would bring him closer to practising our faith with more devotion, but so far my prayers have not been answered — told me that he could feel my restless spirit from his cabin. Moushoom says things like that.

Nothing seemed to help. Perhaps setting my thoughts down on paper will.

So. Monsieur Riel came to our *bal à l'huile* last night. He and his wife had been invited of course, as Papa has known Monsieur Riel since they were both boys back in St. Boniface. It was only Monsieur Riel who arrived, however, not Madame Riel. "Marguerite's cough is plaguing her," he told us. He seemed to enjoy himself, spending a good deal of time talking about his hopes for the Métis people. It was not all seriousness, though. Monsieur Riel and Papa told funny stories about their boyhoods. Both of them were the oldest of eleven children, and there was plenty of opportunity for mischief! I think Papa was the most mischievous, though. It is easy to understand why Armand sometimes behaves the way he does.

But Adrian! He could not take his eyes from Monsieur Riel. All he could speak about this morning was the brilliance of Louis Riel, that he is the leader we have needed, that the government in Ottawa cannot ignore us now. Who better to represent us? He went on about Monsieur Riel sending a petition to the government last month on behalf of the people here — the Indians, the English half-breeds, we Métis and even the whites. Adrian is certain that now Ottawa must give us title to the lands on which we have lived all these years.

Papa agreed. So did I, but then Adrian shouted, "I would follow him anywhere, even if it meant my life."

That is when Moushoom told Adrian to take care, that words sometimes take on a life of their own.

Louis Riel. Some call him our saviour, but I can only imagine what the priests would say to that.

Monsieur Riel is quiet and polite, and he is well educated, having studied at a seminary in Montréal, although he decided against becoming a priest. Before he came here to help with our land problems, he was teaching at a mission school down in the Montana Territory. He does seem like a good man.

I hate to hear Adrian shout. No one shouted that way when Mama was alive. And all over a man he scarcely knows!

Le 7 janvier 1885

Moushoom told me that I should write about interesting newspaper stories in this book. It seems to me that it would be much easier to paste them in with a little flour and water, though. He agreed. I wonder if the newspaper stories are true, since I must put the truth here. Moushoom was quiet for a moment and then said that he doubted that much of anything in the newspapers is true. Still, the stories are interesting to hear.

This is what I decided to paste in. In truth, it was Armand who decided this, because he liked the picture so much. It is easy enough to humour him. Perhaps this schedule is true, although they say the trains cannot ever keep to it. Perhaps they will in time.

CANADIAN PACIFIC RAIL'Y

WESTERN DIVISION

WINTER TIME TABLE

Commencing Sunday, December 7, and until further notice, trains will run as follows: —

Going West				Going East
8:20 a.m.	Leave	Winnipeg	Arrive	6:33 p.m.
11:03 a.m.		Portage la Prairie		4:00 p.m.
3:00 p.m.		Brandon		12:30 p.m.
11:00 p.m.		Broadview		1:15 a.m.
5:25 a.m.		Regina		3:00 p.m.
8:40 a.m.		Moose Jaw		5:20 p.m.
8:10 p.m.		Swift Current		7:55 a.m.
9:40 p.m.		Maple Creek		1:25 a.m.
2:15 a.m.		Medicine Hat		3:13 p.m.
1:30 p.m.		Calgary		5:40 p.m.
1:10 a.m.	Ar.	Leggan	Lv.	5:15 p.m.

Trains between Winnipeg and Brandon daily except Sundays. Three trains a week between Winnipeg and Moose Jaw, leaving Winnipeg Tuesdays, Thursdays and Saturdays; returning leave Moose Jaw Saturdays, Wednesdays and Fridays. Once a week between Winnipeg and Leggan, leaving Winnipeg Tuesday; returning leave Leggan Friday. Train between Calgary and Leggan subject to cancellation at any time without notice.

When I told him that it was too bad the railway had not come to Batoche the way we hoped it might, Moushoom made that sound he makes. He believes that trains are nothing but trouble, with their black smoke and noisy engines.

Moushoom has said many times that people who travel on trains have no sense, that a good horse or a Red River cart is the way Métis travel. One time I reminded Moushoom that his cart and all other Red River carts had to be as noisy as a train, what with the way the wheels squealed so loudly. Moushoom made his sound that time as well.

"The squealing is not noise, Josephine," he said. "It is music!" And I believe he is correct.

Le 8 janvier 1885

Tonight Moushoom told me that he had a story for my diary, one about Louis Riel and our family. It seems that all the talk of travel made him think of it.

He insisted that I write it down exactly as he told it, since there is nothing so important as our family's history. It is part of the Métis history, as closely woven into it as a perfectly worked *saencheur flechee.* Now I will try to do as he asked.

This is what he said:

Les Bouviers in St. Boniface
Told by Moushoom Thompson Bouvier

We came here in '73, as you know. Six head of cattle, we had, five cows and one tough bull. You do not remember riding in the cart though, because you were still in your mother's belly. It was a long sad journey from St. Boniface on the Red River, one we never expected to make, but the government was cutting the land into squares, you see. Surveying for the new white settlers, they said, and there would be no more river lots. All we wanted was title to our land, but a man had to have a piece of *paper* to prove he owned what was his in the first place. That did it for the Bouviers, and the Pepins and so many others, I will tell you. We are *Otipemisiwak,* and no one tells free people how they will live.

Louis Riel spoke for the Métis there, as he is trying to do here now, and some stayed, but not us. In the end, it was not all bad, I suppose. Because of Louis's efforts, the government gave the place a new name. Manitoba. Made it part of Canada. We would keep our Catholic schools for the Métis children, and the Catholic churches were to be left alone. Not so bad maybe — except for the squares of land, which are unnatural. A farm should stretch right on down to the river in a long strip.

Louis, though. He was elected to serve in the Ottawa government three times. He never took his seat, although he did sneak into that parliament building once, and signed the register. And him with a bounty of $5000 on his head to keep him out! *Mafway jeu,* but that must have taken some nerve, all right! Louis went to the States when it was all over. Exile, they called it. I have always thought it was a slap in the face, but on the other hand, I think Louis probably made the correct decision. A wise man always knows when it is a good time to run.

Anyway, we left St. Boniface. You, Josephine, you kicked your mother all the way. When we arrived here in Batoche, you stopped kicking and the next day you were born. Your mother said it was a relief. We claimed a lot along the river, made a home, saw the seasons go by, watched our cattle herd increase.

I watched Moushoom shake his head. "You listen behind doors and through holes in floors while your elders discuss serious matters, Josephine. You want to know everything, but what you may not know is that it is all happening again. Three years ago when those men came with their telescopes? They were surveyors. *Mafway jeu!* Those cursed *squares* again! They want to cut the land — the Métis land — into squares. This will draw even more settlers, like a skinned buffalo carcass draws flies. Not appetizing, but true. I could tell you stories about flies in the old days of the buffalo hunts."

"I know much of this," I told Moushoom.

"Maybe so," he said, "but there is one thing you do not know." When I asked what that thing was, he said, "This time I am certain that Louis Riel will not run."

For some reason those words made me feel uneasy, although I cannot say why.

Le 10 janvier 1885

Madame Brulé is another widow that Papa probably danced with at the Boyers' home that night. She visited this afternoon. Madame did not stay long when I told her that Papa, Moushoom and the boys were out ice fishing. She drank the cup of tea I offered, and then since there is no word for goodbye in Michif, she only said that she would see me again. Cluck, cluck, I nearly answered as I watched her walk away.

Madame Brulé did not leave a *tart de vyawnd,* which is really too bad. Hers are nearly as good as mine.

Le 11 janvier 1885

We stood outside the church and talked after Mass. The widows Laframboise and Brulé would have stood with Papa, I think, except that he was in deep conversation with young Madame Pepin, who came back from Prince Albert last fall for the funeral of her father-in-law. His farm is hers now, although everyone was surprised when she decided to stay, instead of selling the land. She is a Pepin and the Pepins have been in Batoche as long as the Bouviers, but Louise Pepin left Batoche when her husband drowned four years ago. I remember that sad day. Moushoom says, once a Métis from Batoche, always a Métis from Batoche, so that is that.

I cannot imagine running a farm alone. I cannot imagine living away from Batoche for four years, either. True, Madame Pepin did stay with her sister Madame Rose Montour, and I am sure she was a great help in the household, but what would it be like to not have the warmth and comfort of your own kitchen? I pray I never learn that.

Le 12 janvier 1885

We said the rosary together tonight as we almost always do. Later when Armand was ready for bed and I tucked him in, he told me that I must stop the tucking — only a tiny *bābee* is tucked in and he is now six. He no longer believes that *googoosh* — what Emma calls the boogeyman — lives under his bed. Besides, he is starting school for the first time tomorrow. It will be very quiet with him gone, I think.

Le 13 janvier 1885

Papa and Adrian are cutting wood this morning. I mended clothing, mostly Armand's — he tears something almost every day. That same boy who is now too big to be tucked in was also too big to be walked to school by me, I learned. He was just the right size, though, to be walked by Moushoom, with Willow following behind them.

The other dogs stayed in the barn, Bone since she is growing big with puppies and prefers the comfort of her nest, and Moon, perhaps because he is growing old. That he is likely the father of the puppies may also be the reason. Who can understand the mind of a dog?

I am pleased that Armand knows his letters well enough to write his name with chalk on a slate. He is even able to read a little, although the only things he has to read are what I write for him, since we have no books.

I cried to see him go off, but I did it in the quiet of the barn as I collected the eggs. The hens do not care if I cry, after all. Mama, though, would have been so very proud, and that thought is a comfort.

Le soir

It made me smile to hear Armand's stories about school. Père Moulin is strict — they say the nuns who teach downriver in St. Laurent are even stricter — but he is also very kind. Our priest is busy with seeing to our souls, running the post office and teaching children, so I understand why he is strict, what with having to deal with boys like Armand. Yet he is very patient with them. He does not even mind when the boys call him Père Caribou, Armand told us, which is the name many have for him. Papa found this quite funny. Adrian did not, since he believes that a priest deserves much respect. Adrian scowled until Armand announced that he would become a great scholar like Monsieur Riel.

Last year Armand said he wanted to be a buffalo hunter like Moushoom and Papa. Little boys. They are as changeable as the weather.

Le 14 janvier 1885

Today is laundry day. Washing clothing is tedious, but it gives your mind time to think freely. Today I thought about Armand at school and what it would be like to teach. They say that Monsieur Riel's sister Sarah, who was a Grey Nun, taught until she died a year ago. I am not as clever as Père Moulin or Monsieur Riel, but I taught Armand his letters, did I not? Perhaps I will be a teacher one day, although I have no wish to be a nun. I say my prayers faithfully, but I do not think I could pray as often as a nun has to.

Then my soapy hands, working away, made me think about Madame Dumont, and how lucky she is with regard to her laundry. Madame's hands are rough from work just as mine are, but not from washing clothes. She has a washing machine, a most remarkable thing that surely eases her work. Imagine pushing a bar to make one scrub board move across another, scrubbing the clothing that lies between them. Her hands barely touch the water, and to me that would be wonderful. But I should not give in to that sort of envy.

In time, Madame will have a big new house for that washing machine, since Monsieur Dumont is building her one. Perhaps it will be even grander than the Letendres' house, now the finest home in Batoche — two and a half stories tall and with pillars at the front. Gabriel Dumont will have to work very hard to build something grander.

Moushoom thinks grand houses are a waste of wood and time. He also thinks that Madame Dumont's washing machine is strange. He says when he first saw it, the machine made him think of a story, one that had been told to his grandfather by a trapper from Montréal who had wintered at his grandfather's village when Moushoom was a boy. It seems that the trapper's grandmother — it was a very old story — had been washing sheets. She wrung them out and then spread them on the grass for the sun to bleach the linen. They did such things then, the old *Kanayaens* back when Montréal was a new town.

Anyway, she spread the sheets and went back into the house. When she came out later, every sheet had been chewed. How she screamed! Perhaps a bear had attacked the sheets. Her husband must get his gun and shoot it! But then she saw the family goat and noticed a small piece of linen hanging from her mouth. Naturally, the husband did not shoot the goat. The milk was too valuable, even though from that day on it tasted a little of soap.

"What does a goat have to do with Madame Dumont's washing machine?" I once asked Moushoom when he told this story.

"Madeleine Dumont had better watch out," he said. "If that machine chews up Gabriel's breeches, he may shoot it!"

Even now, the thought of that makes me feel like laughing.

Le 15 janvier 1885

Papa and the others went out to hunt this morning with *mo nook* Pierre and *mo nook* Gerard. Both my uncles are very good trackers. Later, when I saw that Papa was not walking home with them, I was afraid, until Edmond told me that Papa had stopped by Madame Pepin's farm. It seems her roof has a leak. I suppose Papa was only being helpful, but it did seem odd that he and no one else offered to patch it.

During supper, I said to Papa that it would not be easy to run a farm alone, or keep house, especially one with a leaky roof. No one had anything to say about that except for Adrian, who remarked that Madame Pepin would not have to worry now. Moushoom began to choke and cough. Papa had to hit him on the back quite a few times. Moushoom eats too fast.

Le 16 janvier 1885

This afternoon I walked to Monsieur Letendre's store with Moon at my side. It was cold and the snow crunched under my boots, but there was no noise from Moon's feet, although he is a big heavy dog. Perhaps it is because he seems so much like a wolf.

When Emma first moved here, she was surprised at how many merchants we have in Batoche. Such a mixture of people. Monsieur Letendre, the Fisher brothers Joseph and Georges, and most of the other merchants are Métis, but Monsieur Garnot is from Quebec, and the Kerr brothers are *li Blawn* from Ottawa. I think it is because they are English that the

Kerrs have not done so well. It takes people here a long time to get used to something new, and to trust it. Monsieur Letendre is trusted. He is also the most prosperous merchant, and because he is sometimes Papa's employer, Papa insists that I shop there. It seems fair to me. It is the least I can do, since Papa works so hard at freighting whenever Monsieur Letendre needs him.

I passed Monsieur Garnot's stopping place. Emma had never heard of such a thing as a stopping place before she came here. When I said that surely in Toronto they had houses where men may stop and take a little drink, where travellers might rest or play billiards and smoke their pipes, Emma put her nose in the air. She told me that in Toronto they are not called stopping places. They are called saloons. I think that stopping place sounds better.

The door was open when I passed, and I could smell tobacco smoke from the men's pipes. Someone called out that Monsieur Garnot needed new felt on his billiard table. That someone was Monsieur Riel. What could anyone expect of a *Kanayah* from Quebec, teased another voice. That one was William Jackson, Monsieur Riel's secretary. Philippe Garnot answered that if they did not like his table, they could play on Georges Fisher's table or maybe on Gabriel Dumont's. Perhaps Métis felt was better. Monsieur Riel laughed at the joke, and I have to admit, it made me laugh as well.

My laughter caused the men to notice me. Someone wondered aloud where my father had been lately. Too busy with other matters to play billiards these days, someone else shouted. Too busy patching leaky roofs. Everyone laughed and poked one another with their elbows. Everyone except Monsieur Riel, who has very nice manners. Now that I think on it, maybe some of them had taken more than a little drink. It was all very odd, and if I hear anything more about a leaky roof, I think that —

Papa is calling me. I will finish later.

Très tard

Papa has asked Louise Pepin to marry him. She agreed. It makes sense, he told me. Her farm lot is next to ours. The house can be rented out in time, once she is living here with us. As well as the income from that, her farm will provide an excellent dowry. Papa has known her for many years and she is a good woman. While he and Adrian are away freighting for Monsieur Letendre, Madame Pepin will be good company for Armand and me. She will be coming to supper tomorrow evening so that we can all welcome her.

I knew Papa would marry again in time, but it

is — I must write this — it is too soon. I smiled sweetly and said that it did make sense, that I was sure she was a good woman, and how convenient that her farm was next to ours. I did not add that her roof no longer leaks.

I held in my tears until I was upstairs, but now I have cried until I can cry no more. Not for my brothers, who all seem pleased by the announcement, or even for myself. I cried for Mama.

No. That is a lie. I *did* cry for myself. How can I bear another woman in my kitchen, in the kitchen where my mother cooked? How can I bear the presence of a woman who will not be a guest, but who will claim the kitchen as her own? I know I cannot.

Encore plus tard

Moushoom knocked on my door an hour ago. He had another story for my book, he explained when I was settled in bed with a shawl around my shoulders. But then he reconsidered and said that maybe this was not the best time for a story. Maybe right now was just a good time to listen.

A man needs a wife, I was told. This I suppose is true, for in the old days, the buffalo-hunt days, a man could not easily hunt without a woman to skin the animals and cut up the meat. True, sometimes the arrangement was *à la façon du pays* until a priest could be found and a proper marriage performed. It was so with my parents, who lived together in the country way until Père André married them. There is no shame in it.

Back then, Moushoom went on, all the women and girls helped with the hunt. For a moment he fell silent. I know what he was thinking just then, and what he could see in his mind. Buffalo, yes, but also the end of a great and wonderful way of life. It made me shiver. I cannot imagine losing such a thing.

My mother, Moushoom told me, had done this before I was born, and maybe some day if the buffalo came back I would do this for my own husband. For now though, I had to help in other ways. Asking Louise Pepin to marry him was not an easy thing for my father to do, and it would not be an easy thing for Louise to come into our family. She would need my help.

How those last five words went against everything I wanted to do!

Then Moushoom reminded me that it always would be my kitchen, just as the house would always be my home, if I was worried about any of that. He was certain I was not, though, since I was a smart girl. And a smart girl knows good advice when she hears it.

I was not so certain about any of that, especially the

last part. He kissed me goodnight, then just before he closed the door he said, "Maybe you should write it down after all so you do not forget it."

Of that, I *was* certain, and so I have.

Le 17 janvier 1885

Louise Pepin came to supper.

Le 18 janvier 1885

When I read back in this diary I can see that I sometimes write the first idea that comes into my head. It is the reason why I have taken time to think carefully about what I want to say about the evening that Louise Pepin came to our house. I have made a vow to think before I write. And before I speak, but I am not certain which will be harder to keep.

So. Louise Pepin did not arrive empty-handed. She brought a loaf of fresh bread and a jar of saskatoon-berry preserves. Our cellar has many such jars of blueberry, saskatoon-berry and bunchberry preserves all put up by me, but I kept that fact to myself and thanked her most graciously. No matter what I was feeling, I would not ever shame my family with bad manners.

We visited. Papa served small glasses of the special wine he makes, his chokecherry *piquette*, adding water to what he gave to Armand and me. Armand made horrible faces at his glass, but Louise did not seem to notice. She told us about life in Prince Albert. It is far too busy there, it seems, and Batoche suited her better. After all, there is a new church here, a school, a post office and enough shops to please anyone. It is good to be home, she said. I have to admit I could understand her feelings about that.

While she talked I studied her and wondered why of all women she should be the one Papa would choose. She is not beautiful, although she has a pleasing smile and, I believe, all of her teeth. I noticed that she is clean and that she had polished her boots. Maybe that was worth something, since she knows nothing about fixing a roof.

Adrian asked her what she thought of Monsieur Riel and before she could answer, he also asked did she not believe he was a great thinker among the Métis people? For a moment, she said nothing. I began to suspect that she had no opinion. But then she said — and I must write it exactly as she said it — "Thoughts come from the mind. The Métis are more than thoughts. There is the heart to consider as well."

I feared there might be an argument because Adrian speaks so highly of Monsieur Riel, even though Louise's words would have been hard to argue against. That was when Moushoom's stomach rumbled. Everyone laughed and Papa said that the supper bell had been rung.

We ate my *grawdpayrs* in chicken broth, a dish of which I am very proud, since they taste just like Mama's. Even Emma enjoys these long, flat dumplings. Louise said she supposed that she would miss browsing through Mister — she used the English word — Mister T. N. Campbell's store back in Prince Albert. There were such fine books in it, she explained, and confessed that now and again she indulged in the purchase of an especially interesting volume. Mister Campbell would send to Montréal for whatever a person wanted. She had heard that I enjoyed books. She would be more than happy to give me the loan of hers.

I am not a child who may be bribed with sweets. Or books.

Plus tard

More. Louise told me that I must call her by her given name. She does not expect to be called *Belmyr,* even though she will be our stepmother.

I still feel the same way about how things are going, but I must admit — only here will I admit it — that for now I have given off trying to find fault with Louise Pepin. At least she has one admirable quality. She enjoys reading when she has a few moments.

Le 19 janvier 1885

Papa enjoys a game of billiards. Since Monsieur Riel has come to Batoche, they sometimes play a game or two at Monsieur Dumont's stopping place. My father says that his friend Louis is a talented opponent, even more skilled than Gabriel is. Papa has described Gabriel Dumont's billiard table to me. He says it is made of mahogany, that it is six feet by twelve feet, and that it is the best table here. The word *Northwest* is engraved on its underside, and although Monsieur Dumont cannot actually read the word, he is very proud of it. Curious that he can speak six languages, yet he does not read or write.

I have never seen that table, though, and I suspect I never will. Papa says that some things are for men and some are for women, and that has always been the way of it here for Métis people. Billiards is not for women, I have been told often enough, which seems unfair, but I suppose Papa is correct. I can scarcely imagine what would happen if I walked into Monsieur Dumont's stopping place and picked up a billiard cue.

The house or the barn and dairy are for women, but I cannot see why the forge should be only for the men. Papa says it is because it is so foul, but I think it is because the forge draws the men the way rug hooking draws the women.

All that may be true, but I like the forge. When the smith hammers the red-hot iron, the sparks look like fireflies. And when his boy pumps the bellows, the fire makes me think of what the *roogaroo's* eyes would look like — if there was such a thing as a trickster that could take the shape of a wolf, that is. There is not.

So. This afternoon after my supper was in the pot and the house in order, I walked to the forge. Moushoom and Papa had been there since late morning, having La Mignonne shoed. She is a good gentle ox, La Mignonne, but not at all the dainty creature her name suggests, and so the blacksmith insists that Moushoom and Papa be there. And Edmond, if he is about, since he is so good with animals. When I arrived, they were just lowering her with the sling used for the task, since like all oxen, she cannot stand upon three legs for long and two shoes are needed for each cloven hoof. What a grunt she gave when all of her new shoes touched the floor!

The smith did not see me, or he would not have chosen the words he used to express his relief. Perhaps this added foulness is another reason that the forge is a not a place for women. I walked in as though he had spoken politely rather than cursing the weight of Bouvier's Monster, as he calls La Mignonne. I kissed her nose and greeted everyone. How Edmond laughed at that.

So did Gabriel Dumont, who was seated with Moushoom, Moïse Ouellette, *mo nook* Napoleon, and my cousin Daniel, watching the work. I asked *mo nook* Napoleon how my cousin Flora was feeling. The poor thing has been suffering terribly from a cough. Well enough, was what he said. Monsieur Dumont made a quiet remark to Edmond in Cree, something about kissing, and laughed harder than ever when Edmond's cheeks reddened. All this I ignored. Instead, I offered to lead La Mignonne home.

"Whoa, boy!" Monsieur Dumont shouted then, observing that I was fearless. Moushoom said it was the Cree blood, not the French blood, that gave me my fearlessness, and the nonsense went on until finally Monsieur Dumont held a newspaper out to me.

"Read this, child," he said, pointing to a page. He gave me the paper, explaining that it was Letendre's paper. Monsieur Letendre had read it to him, and Monsieur Dumont had told Papa what it said, but it would be even better if I read it aloud for all.

This I did, and what an uproar it caused! *Who were these people to make up stories about what goes on here? What was this foolishness? Riel had sent the petition to Ottawa and an answer would come soon. What sort of idiots were these men?*

When the uproar died, Monsieur Dumont said I might keep the paper, seeing that I was a reader like

Madame Pepin. Papa said we must start for home. It was beginning to snow.

And that is what we did.

Plus tard

This is what I read aloud at the forge.

> The Globe's Ottawa correspondent says, "Mr. Chapleau states that Riel has been, to all appearances, very quiet during the summer, but it is well known that he is secretly advising the half-breeds to make a demand upon the Government for compensation for the whole Northwest. Riel's argument is that the whole country belonged to the half-breeds and Indians before the Canadian Government took possession, and that to extinguish the half-breed claim a sum equal to twenty-five cents for every acre of land sold by the Government should be paid them. Perhaps we had all better move out.

Edmond said nothing when I read this story at the forge. As we walked home though, leading La

Mignonne through the falling snow, he wondered aloud how anyone could think to own an entire country.

I agree. All we want is our farm. Surely the government understands that.

Le 21 janvier 1885

Louise has asked Père Moulin which of her books might be suitable for a girl my age. He will examine the titles and make his judgement. I hope there will be even just one.

Le 22 janvier 1885

Armand's stomach hurts. He is not ill, unless you count the illness that comes from a greedy boy eating too much candy. Moushoom has a tin box that he keeps down in the small cellar under his cabin, next to a bottle of brandy he brought from St. Boniface. Now and then Moushoom will give Armand a penny from the box. If my brother saved the pennies he would have something, but instead he buys sweets. Moushoom says he has no use for money, but I wish he too would save his pennies. One never knows.

Le 23 janvier 1885

Strangely mild weather. It makes me think of spring and our sugar bush, although it is far too soon for sugaring, since the sap will not rise for a long while. I can almost taste the snow maple taffy Mama would give us as a treat if we behaved.

Enough writing, Josephine. Sugaring will come in time. For now, there is supper to prepare.

Plus tard

Emma surprised me as I was coming from the cellar, a basket of potatoes and cabbage in my hands. She was able to come over from their home near Duck Lake with her father in their sleigh. He had work to be done at the forge, needing his ploughshare to be straightened and sharpened so it will be ready in spring. The MacLeod land has many rocks and the ploughshare finds them endlessly. Later Emma's father would come here and visit with Papa, who is always happy to give him advice about farming, which is somewhat new to the MacLeods.

I had not known she was coming and so the kitchen was in a state, but Emma does not mind a *rababoo.* That is her favourite Michif word since it is, she says, so very cunning. I cannot see what is cunning about a stew made of vegetables and game meat, but I can see the cleverness of using it to describe a mess. My kitchen was indeed a *rababoo.*

She watched me slice and chop, but all the while I could tell that there was something she wanted to say. My face gives nothing away, I have been told, but Emma's shows all. Finally, out it came. People were saying my father was going to marry Madame Pepin, and she asked if it was true. I admitted that it was true, adding that it made sense. I knew better than to say much more than that. Emma is a friend, but words have a way of growing and changing until they come back to roost like huge chickens filled with gossip. I know those chickens would go to roost in Louise's house, and so I simply said that a wedding is always enjoyable.

Emma then wondered if I had heard about what had been printed in a Toronto newspaper, the very newspaper her father had worked for before they came here. She could not understand how anyone who was not an Indian or a half-breed might have to give up their farm. And she wondered how I could bear being called that — a half-breed. It sounded so common, so very low.

I assured her it meant nothing to me. The name held as much truth as the newspaper story did, and that was little indeed. Her father's sleigh arrived just then. Papa met it, her father climbed down, and the two men began to walk to the house. Emma said nothing more about the matter.

Encore plus tard

The word has tumbled about in my head most annoyingly, like a bit of fiddle music that will not stop, until finally here I am out of bed.

Half-breed. In our family, only Moushoom is half of one people and half of another, his mother having been Cree and his father a *Kanayah* from Québec. And what about me? Mama's great-grandmother was of the Sarcee people. Is one of my ears then *Kanayaen* and the other Cree, and if so, which is which? Do I have a Sarcee nose or a French nose? I am certainly not half of one thing and half of another, but that is what I will always be called, it seems. If I have children some day, I wonder if it will be the same for them?

Mama once said that we Bouviers are like threads in a long, tightly woven sash — and as difficult to unravel. One thing I do know. I may be made up of many things, but I am entirely Métis.

Le 24 janvier 1885

Bone's puppies were born in the night. All but one perished of the cold, or perhaps from her lack of experience. Poor things. Emma will be so disappointed, as she was hoping to have a puppy from this litter.

Moushoom brought all the dogs and Bone's living puppy into the house. Moushoom has named the puppy Eagle, since he is strong. His dogs do not have fleas, he says, but I am glad they sleep with him and not me.

I wonder what Louise will make of a houseful of dogs?

Le 25 janvier 1885

Louise brought a book here this evening. It is called *Les Contes de Perrault,* and it has ten stories with pictures. The stories all have morals, and that is especially good. It seems that Père Moulin says they will be acceptable for me to read, all except for one story called "La Barbe-Bleu." It is far too frightening for a girl my age, and he advises me to avoid it. How a tale about a man with a blue beard could be frightening is very odd. Moushoom laughed and laughed at this, saying it would take more than a blue beard to frighten his Josephine.

Plus tard

Louise is fond of dogs, especially puppies.

Au point du jour

Moushoom was wrong. "La Barbe-Bleu" was terrifying! I wish I had not read that horrible, horrible story. The fact that it had a moral — curiosity, in spite of its appeal, often leads to deep regret — does not help at all.

I must vow to be less curious!

Le 26 janvier 1885

Big Tom Hourie passed through Batoche today, travelling southeast to Qu'Appelle. This always results in many comments. Monsieur Hourie is a tall man, well over six feet. Armand thinks he is an English half-breed giant.

Papa says Tom Hourie is not English at all, although he is a half-breed. His ancestor came from an island near a country called Scotland many years ago to work for the Hudson's Bay Company, and this man took a wife from among the Snake people.

All Moushoom says is that Tom Hourie is too tall for his own good, but he only says that to be funny.

I wonder what it is like, working for the English. It must be a strange thing, no matter how tall or short you are.

Le 27 janvier 1885

We will have rabbit for supper tonight. There were eight of them in Edmond's snares. Moushoom has salted the skins and set them aside to be tanned, so that I may use them to line moccasins. There is nothing like rabbit fur against your bare feet.

Plus tard

Moushoom has often said that tanning a hide is more than preserving a skin, that it is almost as though you are giving life to the animal once again. He reminded me of this as he and I worked on the skins this afternoon, stretching them and scraping away every bit of flesh and fat.

It set me to thinking. I make three pairs of moccasins for everyone in our family each year, just as Mama did. Mine are not as fine as hers were, since the beadwork on the Sunday moccasins is simpler, but they are comfortable. Emma and her family buy boots that they wear summer and winter, and none of them own even one pair of moccasins. I think that must be a very hard way to walk through life.

Le 28 janvier 1885

We had unexpected guests today, or rather Moushoom did. It was Louis Riel and Gabriel Dumont. All this month Monsieur Riel has been visiting families around here, but Papa says it is more than just visiting. Monsieur Riel wants to know what men such as Moushoom and my father are thinking. When Adrian added that Monsieur Riel was seeking out not just any men, but important and influential men, Papa only shrugged. My father is a very modest man.

The visit, though. Adrian, Edmond and Papa were adding some chinking to the logs of Moushoom's cabin, and I was there preparing rabbit soup for all of them. Moushoom has an old stove in his cabin, one called a Carron stove that he brought with him, strapped to the back of his cart, when our family came from St. Boniface. Years before that, the stove had travelled even farther. It was made in the country of Scotland, and had been brought across the ocean on a ship.

My grandfather was saying that food tastes better when it is cooked on that stove, when we heard the sound of horses and voices. Moments later, in came the visitors. There was enough soup for six hungry men and one girl, but only just.

They ate in silence, all crowded into the cabin. I suppose some would say that I should have gone back to the big house. This was men's business, after all. But I did not. Why should I? Mama would have stayed, as she had always taken a keen interest in the affairs of Batoche. But Monsieur Riel had not come on business. He and Gabriel Dumont had come to offer my family their congratulations regarding Papa's forthcoming marriage.

That done, Monsieur Dumont pointed to me,

telling Monsieur Riel that this was the girl who could read English newspapers — thanks to her sainted mother Anne, may she rest in peace.

"Josephine is as well-educated a girl as Batoche has ever seen," Moushoom boasted, adding that he had given me a diary some months back and that I am an excellent writer. Moushoom and Monsieur Dumont are given to exaggerations, but I smiled anyway.

Monsieur Riel said that I must be a comfort to my father, that education is a blessing, and that reading and writing are a gift. He said that he sometimes writes poetry, and is even writing a novel, one called *Masinahican*. It is the Cree word for book, he explained, when Moushoom told him that I speak very little Cree. Monsieur Riel went on to say that he keeps a journal himself, a thing he considers to be a very important activity. As for stories, a story should be written down to pass on, he told me. I am doing a fine thing.

Not long after this, all the men left the cabin. I could hear them talking outside as I stacked up the bowls, but I could not make out what they were saying. Later Adrian told me that I should be very honoured by Monsieur Riel's words, that he is a remarkable man. Was I aware that some call him the father of Manitoba?

Papa said to Adrian that perhaps Louis was a

remarkable man — time would tell. He is sure that Monsieur Riel wants the best for the Métis people, just as he wants the best for his children — like any good father.

I am lucky to have Papa, and I suppose Monsieur Riel's children are lucky to have him.

Le 29 janvier 1885

Still and very cold. I could see a fog of tiny ice needles hanging in the air. So beautiful and peaceful. Unlike the inside of the house, although I am not complaining, since it rings with Armand's laughter. Only a little boy could laugh so hard at a tiny puppy's fat belly.

Le 30 janvier 1885

Edmond shot a mule deer today when they were out hunting, a large buck that still wore its antlers. Armand was very cross that he missed the excitement. He had been at school. When I teased that learning to read was also quite exciting, he began to pout until Edmond told Armand that he would make him a fine knife handle from part of one of the antlers. Edmond spoils that boy.

Emma hates to see a kill. She hides her eyes and makes the sound of vomiting. Even I think this is strange. I have always been told that animals give themselves willingly to a hunter if the animal is treated with respect. Papa thinks it may be so, but Moushoom and Edmond truly believe it. I suppose that is because they both lived among the Cree as children, and still cling to Cree ways and beliefs. That is how they see things. Père Moulin does not see it that way, of course.

What I see is a fine fat mule deer. They will butcher him and share out some of the meat.

Le 31 janvier 1885

Moushoom went over to One Arrow today with a haunch of venison. He was quiet for a long while upon his return. I knew why. Times are hard here, but it is far worse for the Cree on that reserve.

Le 1 février 1885

Père Moulin read the first of the banns in church this morning, naming my father and Louise, asking if anyone knew of any reason why these two should not be joined in marriage. I will not write down what my first thought was at that moment. I should have prayed for acceptance, but I could not.

It was far too windy to linger outside the church very long afterward, but that did not stop people from congratulating Papa and Louise. I was not neglected. All of the girls I know, girls who look forward to their own marriages in time, said that I must be so pleased. A wedding! They *loved* a wedding! What could I do but agree?

Le 4 février 1885

I have been unwell with a cough that has been bothering me now and again, especially at night. Coneflower tea helps a bit, but until now, writing has been beyond me.

I know it worries Papa greatly when any of us cough. The coughing sickness takes so many people, but I assured him this is only a cough from a cold, not what Emma calls consumption. There is no blood on my handkerchief.

None of us can forget what Mama's cough was like near the end. She was so ill, and suffered greatly, but she could not bear to let go of us.

It was so hard to let her go. I know that I should not dwell on those last days, but there are times when I do. Even in the last hours of her life I could see the love in her eyes. And I cannot help but to think about Madame Riel, who coughs a great deal and has seemed so weary each time I have seen her.

Le 5 février 1885

Tonight after supper, Moushoom talked a little about the reserve. It took him a few days to settle his mind about what he had seen, I suppose, as well as to loosen his unwilling tongue. The small glass of brandy that Papa poured for him also helped some.

Kah-pah-yak-as-to-cum — the English call him Chief One Arrow — had sent his greetings and his congratulations that Papa was taking another wife. He also sent thanks for the venison. He wondered why I had not come to see him in such a long while, but then he supposed I was too busy eyeing the young men of Batoche. It would please him to see me again before he died, not that he was dying soon, but he was an old man, after all. Moushoom seemed to find that very funny. Not the part about dying, but that One Arrow is an old man. He is only seventy and Moushoom is almost eighty.

Moushoom told us that the people there are nearly broken. There is hunger, of course, but they have lost much more since the buffalo have refused to come. The Cree are willing to farm, even though they are not farmers, and yet that is what Macdonald in Ottawa expects them to be. And with no help!

Moushoom looked ready to spit at the very thought of it. He often spits when he talks about the prime minister, but he remembered that he was in the house and did not.

"Lucky Métis," he went on. "At least we have a little French farmers' blood in our veins. Unlucky Cree with none. They are not eating their dogs yet, though."

Moushoom has sometimes talked about having to eat the dogs and some of the horses in '25. That was a bad year for the buffalo hunt. It broke his heart to eat his dogs, even though the dogs were willing. He could not do it now, he says, weak old man that he has become.

I always have to force myself not to smile at those words, since Moushoom is anything but weak.

When Moushoom and Edmond went back to the cabin, Papa said it was odd how the old days, even the bad ones, can seem so real.

I think so too.

Le 6 février 1885

I baked today, and sent some *galet* over to the MacLeods with Adrian, who was taking time to visit Emma. It was a good thing that Armand was at school, since he now chants *nichimoose* at Adrian whenever he learns there is to be a visit. I do think they may be sweethearts, though, if only a little.

Louise has told us that there is a bakery in Prince

Albert where her sister buys all her bread and cakes. There is no *galet* in that bakery, though, so what use is it? Louise had hoped that her sister Rose would be able to come to Batoche for the wedding. She wrote to her some time ago, but today Louise learned that this will not happen. Madame Montour is again with child, and so is not allowed to travel. This order comes from her doctor.

I must admit that secretly I feel a little sorry for Louise, but she has only said that one must accept such minor disappointments. The big ones are hard enough to bear. Besides, she has plenty of cousins here.

Odd. Mama used to say the same sort of thing about disappointment. I wonder how she would feel about Louise.

Plus tard

I have been thinking about Mama and Rose Montour. Mama came all the way here with me in her belly, and that was no small thing, since riding in a Red River cart is a bumpy affair. Perhaps Madame Montour is a delicate woman. She must be, if she is unable to travel here, or perhaps it is because of living in the city. I have heard that a city can change a person, make them softer, more needful of easy living.

Batoche is no city. Life here certainly is not easy, and there is nothing soft about the Bouviers.

Still, I wonder if I would have the courage and strength to cross a prairie with a *bābee* inside me. Moushoom thinks I should not worry about things of that nature. There is time enough to find out just how strong I am, he says. Life will see to that.

Le 7 février 1885

Papa thinks it is a good idea for Louise to send over some of her father-in-law's household things. I could not see why, but I did not argue. There is room, I suppose, and so today Edmond took the sleigh and brought back a load of objects wrapped in newspaper.

When we unwrapped the objects we found several stoneware jugs, a few crocks and even a pot for herbs, all of which will be useful, I have to admit.

What they were wrapped in was better, though, six sheets of newspaper from the *Qu'Appelle Vidette.* Even though the pages were from last December, they were still of interest. Everyone roared with laughter when I read this aloud to hear what people there take for news.

———————<>———————

LOCAL HAPPENINGS

"Mr. Fawcett" will appear next week.

Large amounts of grain are coming in daily, which makes times lively in town.

Skating is the fashionable amusement in town. The ice is in splendid condition.

A son of Antoine LaRocque was knocked down by a boar last Sunday and severely hurt.

During the past week we have been blessed with the most delightful weather.

The prizes awarded at the agricultural show will be paid at the office of T.W. Jackson, Esq., Fort Qu'Appelle, upon demand.

About thirty teams have been engaged in this neighborhood to carry Indian supplies to the south branch of the Saskatchewan.

None of us could think of any fashionable amusement that happened here at Batoche. Maybe mucking out stables, Adrian suggested. Moushoom wondered about a town where the coming in of grain made it lively. And he for one did not ever want to go back to Qu'Appelle again if it meant being trampled by a boar.

Then his expression changed and he wondered if any of that grain had ever made it to the reserve here. He would ask One Arrow.

Armand wanted to make up stories about our household. I suggested that since it was Saturday, the stories would be about taking a bath in the washtub. He did not laugh at that. Armand is not fond of bathing.

Plus tard

It makes me feel strange to see Louise's things in this house. They now stand on the shelves in between Mama's crocks and pots. It is almost as though they are trying to come between Mama and me, somehow.

Le 8 février 1885

Papa, Louise and Père Moulin set a date for the wedding last night, and the second of the banns was read this morning. They will be married the day after the last banns are read next Sunday, so that they do not have to wait until the end of Lent. The word spread after Mass, as word will. There were more congratulations. Madame Riel spoke with Louise. She had been absent from Mass last week and so had been unable to give her best wishes until now.

But the marriage was not the most important topic. There was a rumour that a telegram arrived from the government concerning the petition Monsieur Riel sent in December. But like most rumours it had many faces. Some said the news was very good. Others said nothing good ever came from Ottawa. Papa said that it would be best to just wait and see, nothing was to be gained by guessing.

Monsieur Riel shook Papa's hand and said something to him, something I did not hear because of the way the women were laughing and chattering. Men's talk, I suppose.

Le 9 février 1885

It seems the rumours were true. Edmond heard it all today at the forge, how the telegram had been given to Monsieur Nolin, who showed it to Monsieur Riel last night. Monsieur Riel had been furious. So was Adrian as we listened to Edmond's account. Even Papa, who is always so calm, was uneasy.

The government will investigate the Métis' complaints, they say. But what more is there to investigate? They have known of our complaints for years. They know we want title to our river lots, that what we need is *proof* of ownership. How can they not agree to say that what is ours is ours? Riel is said to have shouted that Ottawa would have his answer in forty days.

"Sounds like a Métis flood is coming," Moushoom said under his breath.

Le 10 février 1885

This morning as I gathered the eggs — the hens were warm and sleepy, and so pecked little — I heard the sound of horses. There was also the sound of our dogs barking, for they are excellent watchdogs. "Someone must be here," I shouted to Edmond, who was milking one of our goats.

"Three men, all mounted," he answered.

I always find this sort of comment very amusing. Edmond insists he can tell what is coming from the sound alone, as his Cree grandfather could. "What colour are the horses?" I asked, as I always do. Edmond did not have anything to say about that. He never does.

When we walked out of the barn, though, a basket of eggs in my arms and a pail of milk in each of Edmond's hands, there were the three horses tied to our hitching rail. I did not have to look at Edmond to know he was smiling at his own cleverness. I asked if he knew the horses' names and he said, "Gabriel Dumont."

"What an odd name for a horse," I teased, but of course he meant that one of the horses belonged to Monsieur Dumont.

"That white left forefoot," Edmond pointed out. "Gabriel's horse." We both could guess at least one of the other owners.

Gabriel Dumont sat at our kitchen table with my father and grandfather. So did Louis Riel and Charles Nolin. Adrian leaned against the wall. I could smell the *kinikinik* Moushoom was smoking, the familiar mixture of red willow bark and bearberry leaves. The guests nodded when I asked if they wanted a little barley coffee. I smiled to myself, since their thirst would give me a chance to listen to their conversation. But they spoke only of the weather, and of cattle, and of the expensive English shotguns in Mitchell's store over at Duck Lake. Two buffalo skulls hang over the door there. Monsieur Dumont wondered who had actually shot those buffalo. He must ask Mitchell how a fancy English shotgun would perform against a buffalo.

They sipped their coffee in silence, and then Monsieur Riel asked, "You are with us then, Michel?" There was something about the way he asked it, as though it was the most important question in the world.

Papa looked at me and I could tell he was very close to sending me upstairs. Papa tries to protect me. He did not send me up, though. He glanced at Adrian, who clearly wanted to shout once more that he would follow Monsieur Riel anywhere. As for Moushoom, he sat very still. Only the smoke from his pipe moved around him.

Then Papa answered that yes, he was with them in expecting justice, in expecting title to the farm, as were his father and son. But none of them were violent men, any more than Louis was. This they must understand.

It seemed to satisfy the visitors, and so they thanked me for the coffee and went on their way.

It had not satisfied Adrian, though. I can hear him arguing with Papa.

Plus tard

I was unable to sleep. When I went downstairs, Adrian had gone to bed, but Papa and Moushoom were sitting near the stove. Papa was mending harness, while Moushoom worked on a sash he had begun just before Mama died. He insists that it will be his last *saencheur flechee,* and he often says that he wants to be buried with it wrapped around his waist.

When he repeated this yet again, Papa told Moushoom not to be so gloomy — he was no more near death than One Arrow was, and besides, we had more important things to talk about than what he would wear at his own funeral.

Papa told me to sit down, and Moushoom stopped weaving for a moment, letting the wool hang from his fingers. When he said that he had the feeling another story for my book was coming, I had to laugh. He was correct, though, and so I have written Papa's words here as well as I can recall them:

"You remember when Gabriel Dumont, Moïse Ouellette and the others went down to Montana to get Louis Riel last summer, to ask him to come up here and speak to the government on our behalf? Louis had been teaching school down there, living a nice quiet life with his wife and children. A good man, loyal to his family and to his people. I think it must have suited him after all that happened in Manitoba fifteen years ago, when we stood up for what was ours. Louis is a hard one to understand, unlike Gabriel. Gabriel is as easy to read as . . . as . . . "

Here he slowed down, trying for the right words.

"As easy to read as the track of a bull buffalo?" asked Moushoom helpfully.

Papa laughed. "Yes. Gabriel is like a bull buffalo, all shaggy, determined and strong. Louis is more like a raven with his black hair and quick mind. You never know with a raven, just how his mood will go. Bring up religion or politics around Gabriel and that is one thing, but bring them up to Louis and —

whoa, boy! Like throwing brandy on a fire."

"Which," Moushoom said, "would be a waste of good brandy."

"Louis Riel means to act if the government refuses to respect the rights of the Métis people," Papa went on. "He has the support of many around here, even the English, although I am not so certain of that these days." Then he looked right at me. "We have to be ready for changes, Josephine. Yes, there is Louise, but she is not what I mean. This marriage means a change that I have brought upon us by my own choice, and it will result in good things for the family."

That is when Moushoom spoke up, saying that this other thing though, this matter of title to our land, and what will be done if we are driven to the edge of the cliff, is a different matter. Moushoom shook his fist and cried that it *is* our land, that no one, especially Macdonald, should think otherwise. Sadly though, Moushoom could not say what was coming.

"Your brother and grandfather and I are with Louis Riel," said Papa. "Adrian's blood is up, but that is Adrian — nothing happens quickly enough for him, and so the arguing. Ignore that, Josephine. What you need to know is that this family stands together, and with God's blessing and a little patience, we will continue to live peacefully."

The thought of peace *should* make my mind feel easier. Still, Moushoom's words will not leave my thoughts. He cannot see what is coming, but I fear that peace has nothing to do with it. Papa. He tries so hard to keep me from worrying.

Au point du jour

I dreamed of falling, moments ago, and it was an awful thing. I had slipped off the edge of a cliff, and went spinning out, falling and falling, unable to breathe because I was afraid of smashing onto the ground. I woke just before that happened, though, thank *Le Boon Jeu.*

I did not really want to write down the last part of last night's story, but I can see that I must. The story needs its ending, after all, and perhaps the writing will keep the dream from coming back.

So. When Papa finished speaking, Moushoom reminded him that some people — the Blackfoot people, if he was not mistaken — used to drive buffalo to the edge of a cliff. It was during a time when the Blackfoot had no guns. It all ended the same way, though. The buffalo would fall to their deaths.

Last night I did not think it was a very cheerful ending for the story, but there it was. Now, though, I believe my grandfather had not been talking about buffalo at all.

Le 11 février 1885

I have helped Papa move the last of Mama's belongings from his room into mine. There was not much, only some clothing, and a small hooked rug she was working on before she died. Papa held her diary, the one she had begun when they left St. Boniface. He said it was foolishness for him to keep it, as he cannot read. I told him it was not. Besides, it would be all he had left of Mama.

"You should have it," he said, and he pressed the diary into my hands. "You and the boys are part of what I have left of Mama." Then he put one of his own hands over his heart. "The rest — the memories, and the love — will always be here, Josephine." It took all my strength not to weep.

Perhaps I will finish Mama's rug, but I am not certain I can ever bring myself to read her diary.

Le 12 février 1885

Even though it is her wedding, Louise has offered to help me make preparations for the celebration to follow. She would cook and bake in the kitchen of her father-in-law's house, naturally. I said yes.

Louise is a good woman, but I treasure these last days that this kitchen is mine alone. It is the place where Mama was the happiest, and sometimes I can almost feel her near me. Will I still feel that when Louise is here? It saddens me that I may not.

Le 13 février 1885

A pleasant happy day. We journeyed out this morning, two of our horses pulling our sleigh. Edmond had the reins and I sat beside him with my grandfather behind us, a small sack of venison at his feet. In Moushoom's arms was his Winchester 66 rifle. He treasures it so, and has named it *Gárso Zhounn* — his yellow boy. It is a clever name, because of the rifle's brass parts, but then Moushoom is clever with words.

Out we went past the garden, past the barn with its chickens, cats and our goats, across the small hay field and the open pasture where our cattle pawed the snowy ground looking for a bit of last summer's grass. Winter is hard on the animals, but our cattle are tough. It takes more than winter to bother Bouvier cattle. The wind was harder on this Bouvier, I fear, and I could not help but think of our house and its warm kitchen, even though the place we were heading to would also be warm. Two miles is not so far to ride.

Then, there it was. I felt the same odd flutter inside me that I always feel when I see the reserve. It is called Une Flèche, after Moushoom's friend,

Chief One Arrow. Again I felt that flutter inside me, because these are Moushoom's people and Edmond's, the Willow Cree. Mine as well, I suppose, since there is Cree blood in my veins.

I saw one woman moving between the tipis with a load of sticks in her arms, but everyone else was inside. All the tipis faced east and so we could not yet see the fronts, but I knew that the door flaps would all be snugly closed against the wind. There were no barns or stables here, and so the horses took what shelter they could between some Red River carts standing near the tipis.

We stopped at One Arrow's tipi, our horses content to wait quietly while we visited. One Arrow's horses were there too, and all the horses nickered and talked to each other, the way horses do. This tipi was painted just as all the others were, and yet somehow One Arrow's tipi looked like that of a chief. The images were faded, but they still told the story of his life. Here he was going into battle on horseback, armed with a bow and arrow, protected only by a buffalo-hide shield. Here he was hunting buffalo, his horse close to the stampeding bull. There were other animals and scenes that meant little to me. I had been told that these were dreams that mean a great deal to One Arrow, though.

In we went. One Arrow would have been told of our approach, but he shouted out in surprise anyway, and gestured for Moushoom to sit next to him in a place of honour near the rear of the tipi. The shouting makes for a better welcome. He called Moushoom by his Cree name, Mihkwânikwacâs. Moushoom had dark red hair as a boy, so the name Red Squirrel is fitting, although his hair is white now.

It makes me think about Moushoom's other name, which is more difficult to understand. Thompson — Thompson Bouvier — because he was born the year that an English man the Cree called Koo-Koo-Sint came to look at the stars and wintered near a village where Moushoom's parents were staying. His English name was David Thompson, this man who worked for The North West Company of traders. All three are still Moushoom, but no one calls him Thompson.

But back to the visit. Moushoom gave One Arrow's daughter the gift of meat. She immediately began to serve us bowls of food. I remembered how Moushoom had said that the people here were close to starving. Still, we could not refuse. That would have been rude, and so there I sat eating the stew.

You would think a tipi would be cold in the winter, that fourteen or fifteen buffalo hides would never keep out the cold, but they do. Besides, the tipi had a warm inner lining and a cozy fire burning on the ground at its centre. I soon felt quite warm.

I do not speak Cree as well as I might, and so I

simply listened and smiled at the women while the men talked. Like my grandfather, though, Edmond speaks Michif, French and Cree. I do not mind them speaking Cree except when they use it as a secret language to keep things from me. I know a few words, but not enough to discover their secrets.

Finally, One Arrow leaned over to me and held out a finely painted *parfleche.* Inside the leather packet was a gift of pemmican for my father and his new wife, Moushoom explained, made after the last buffalo hunt. I knew the mixture of meat, fat and berries would be at least five years old, but of course pemmican will keep much longer than that.

I was told that One Arrow said I was becoming a fine young woman. I smiled modestly. I was also told that the next time we came here One Arrow would no longer be able to stop his young men from asking for me in marriage. I did not smile at that. How could I? Moushoom laughed and said it was in fun, that One Arrow still had his old sense of humour. Besides, One Arrow knew that the Métis liked to wait until their women were almost too old before they married. It was unfortunate. He said I looked content, that the prospect of having another woman in the house seemed to agree with me. Marriage meant babies, he went on, and more work for the women, but that was a good thing — it was important to keep busy.

Suddenly One Arrow looked very sad, and Moushoom explained that the chief still mourned the loss of a grandchild. One Arrow's wish for us was that our family would never have to do the same.

I thought about that all the way home.

Plus tard

Armand was very cross that he had missed the outing today, saying that going to the reserve was more important than school. He made me describe everything, and so I turned the description into a story. At its end, Armand said he wants to draw pictures on the outside of our house, so that it looks like One Arrow's tipi. He was not pleased when I said he would do no such thing. "No one can stop me," he shouted.

I wonder if Louise understands just how stubborn Armand can be? *Abain,* I suppose she will find out soon enough.

Le 14 février 1885

I wonder how I could have become such a foolish girl with such a shameful habit as listening to private conversations. But if I did not, how would I ever learn anything? And so last night I listened at the floor hole while Papa and Moushoom talked.

Papa wondered if it had been a good thing for me

to go out to the reserve. Some people still have bad feelings about the disagreement between the Cree and the people of Batoche regarding the land boundaries separating the reserve and us, he said. Moushoom told Papa that land is one thing. Respect for Mihkwânikwacâs's granddaughter is another. And that was that.

They talked about Chief One Arrow, and what he had said. One Arrow still had the silver medal he had received from signing a treaty. He was proud of that medal since it signified his bond with the Queen. But sometimes it seemed as though the medal was as cold as the hearts of the men who had given it to him. The government had not kept their promises, no matter what they had said.

Moushoom said that One Arrow still has regrets about the treaty — it was hard to go against the Cree way of life, which was following the buffalo, not digging the earth.

Then Moushoom mentioned something else — that One Arrow likes Riel and Dumont, enjoys their company when they come to visit him. He will not turn his back on friendship or blood.

Papa said that he had a sense that something very bad was coming for both the Cree and us. "It is a pity that the prime minister cannot see what life is like here, how the Métis way is threatened by all the settlers who will be coming here. Why can we not be left alone in our own country?"

Moushoom said some very rude words, the same ones that I had heard at the forge. He said them in Cree, which made them sound even worse. Then he reminded Papa of what Macdonald had said back in the days when they lived at St. Boniface, that the French half-breeds were determined to keep the North West a buffalo reserve forever. Did that sound like a wise man who cared about the Métis way of life? And Moushoom grumbled another rude word.

I could not make out Papa's answer, but I myself thought that Macdonald did not sound wise at all. And it frightens me that Papa has a bad feeling about what will happen.

Le 15 février 1885

Père Moulin read the last of the banns this morning. Papa and Louise will be married tomorrow.

Plus tard

A very small dog has been drawn on the outside back wall of Moushoom's cabin. I suppose I should wash it off, but I have decided to leave it there, at least for a while. After all, Moushoom likes dogs, and so does Louise.

Le 16 février 1885

Au point du jour

Sleep is impossible. Prayer has not helped. I am a selfish girl who thinks of nothing but herself, and who cares only for her own happiness.

There. Tell the truth, Moushoom said to me, and maybe this is the truth.

Mama's watch lies on the table here, next to my diary. I will wear it today tied around my neck with a long ribbon so that it rests over my heart. *For Anne Bouvier, Batoche, 1872, on the occasion of the birth of our daughter, Josephine. My love for all time, Michel,* is what is inscribed on its back. I know these words and the truth that is part of them. Papa will always love and remember her.

The last truth is that I love Papa very much. If this marriage makes him happy, then so be it, but it will be hard, so very hard.

Plus tard

Papa and Louise's wedding was beautiful, which I suppose should be a comfort to me. There were no flowers, of course, but we had decorated the altar with boughs of spruce and the church smelled like a forest. Louise wore a new blue dress with dozens of small buttons down the front, the hem trimmed with lace. Papa wore his best deerskin coat, one that Mama embroidered for him long ago. Almost everyone in Batoche attended, and for once Armand did not wiggle. I wept, but there were so many happy tears that mine went unnoticed. After the wedding we went home, and when the kitchen was filled with friends and family we sang.

Nous sommes ici a soir
Assisses à votre table
Salut la compagnie
Aussi la mariée.

How many times have I heard that song in people's homes after weddings? Here we were tonight, all of us around the table, toasting everyone, but especially the newly married couple. It is a very happy song.

There was a big cake, three layers high. And there was a small package from Madame Montour. It contained a note, which Louise read to herself, and then to all of us. Her sister sent her love and best wishes as well as a *médaille miraculeuse* and a chain for it. It was a very beautiful silver medal showing the Virgin Mary, her hands outstretched in blessing. Louise put it on immediately.

As for the celebration, I am sure I can say that everyone was here. Our house was filled to overflowing with friends and family. Even Moushoom's dogs were in attendance, and all were well behaved except for Eagle, who behaved no worse than Armand, I suppose. Puppies and boys will play noisily, but it was a happy noise. And I even had a chance to visit with my cousins Veronique and Henriette, when I was not helping serve the guests. Emma as well, since she and her parents were here helping us celebrate. The Riels attended for a short while, although Monsieur Riel spent most of his time talking with other men rather than dancing. Madame Riel did not dance either, saying it just made her cough more. She did seem to enjoy watching the dancers, though.

That was not the case with me. I danced until my feet tingled with it, and then I danced more. The rabbit dance, *la danse du crochet,* the duck dance and a great many Red River jigs. Our house rang with the sounds of *turtulage* as people tapped spoons or their toes and heels to the music. Mouth harps and fiddles joined in. When the pitch of the fiddle music was lowered, women or men took turns adding fancy changes to their jigging and, although all were good, Edmond's changes were the best and the quickest. It was no surprise. He is Edmond Swift Fox, after all!

When Papa said later that the celebration was not too bad as such things went, Louise simply rolled her eyes. Moushoom said it was unfortunate that it had only lasted one day, since a wedding celebration should last three, but we had celebrated three times as hard, so it would do. Papa agreed that it was a shame to cut it short, but it was important that we take part in the prayers at St. Laurent tomorrow. Monsieur Riel had reminded him of this a number of times.

Tomorrow is *Laenjee Graw* — even Emma calls this by its French name, *Mardi Gras* — which will be followed by *Zhour di Sawndr* as it is every year. Normally we would visit and feast to mark the last day before Lent. Instead, we will pray. Changes. So many changes.

Encore plus tard

That *médaille miraculeuse* has started me thinking, which is the worse thing I can do at this time of night. It is just that the Blessed Mother is the patron of childbirth. A brother or sister will come in time, I suppose.

I recall the night that Armand was born, and Nohkom LaBute came to act as midwife. Nohkom — she is not my grandmother, but everyone calls her that — said that I was a lucky girl. Bouvier women always had an easy time of bringing their children into the world. I can remember thinking that the whole thing had not seemed so easy to me, but I kept that to myself.

Childbirth can be so difficult. Many women do not survive, and sometimes neither does the *bābee.* Perhaps it is a good thing that Louise has that medal.

Le 17 février 1885

The prayers at St. Laurent de Grandin church lasted forty hours, although we were only there for a few of them. I was glad that Armand had not come along, as the cold wind made the twelve miles there and back seem much farther. Poor Armand had a fever and tightness in his breathing, and so stayed home with Moushoom and Edmond. I rubbed some of my goose grease on his chest, and ordered him to bed with one of his favourite toys, the *bonhomme jigueur* that Papa made for him last year. He loves the way the *jigueur's* arms and legs dance around. Eagle tucked himself in against Armand's side as though to say, "There, boy. Now you will be warm!" Then off we went.

Though St. Laurent church is a small building that can hold perhaps sixty people at most, we had left the house very early and so were able to get seats. My eyes were closed and my rosary was in my hands when I heard Père Fourmond say that he wished to read something. It was something that had been written by Monsieur Riel, a prayer dedicating the Métis people to the Sacred Heart of Jesus. It asked that we be given light and protection and strength, and that we who are united by blood be saved.

It was a prayer of great feeling, and of all the times of the year, I think that Lent is when we pray hardest to be protected and saved from evil. Yet now it makes me wonder. What sort of evil might Monsieur Riel have been thinking about when he wrote that?

Le 18 février 1885
Zhour di Sawndr

Since Emma and her family are not Catholics, they do not observe Lent the same way we do. They are Presbyterian — I must ask her about the spelling of that word — and they would have to go all the way to Prince Albert or to Qu'Appelle for church each Sunday. That is simply too far, especially in winter.

Emma's mother misses their church back in Toronto. St. Andrew's it is called. She is also homesick and longs for her family terribly, writing letters that are taken away by the mail carrier every two weeks. Emma says that once her mother even sent a telegram from the office downriver at Clarke's Crossing, even though it was very costly. Sending words through a wire. It is such a strange idea.

Emma's family will continue to eat meat on

Fridays as they always do. All of our Fridays are meatless, of course, and so it is a good thing that I like fish. We might also have muskrat and duck, if our men are fortunate enough to get any, for those creatures spend so much time in the water that their flesh is not really meat. And we will fast, taking only one full meal most days until Lent is complete.

I have tried to imagine homesickness, and I cannot. It must be a hard thing to never see your home again.

Le 19 février 1885

Very mild weather today. Thanks to the tea that Louise brewed for him from spruce needles, cherry and balsam bark, Armand feels much better. Still, he stayed home from school and it was left to me to try and amuse him with card games, but Armand cannot seem to grasp euchre. He could make buildings with the cards though, and that was good enough.

That let me work on Mama's rug. I got out her bag of rags and picked up her hook. How the memories flooded in, and how the tears threatened to do the same, but I forced them back. I would not let myself cry in front of Louise.

I can remember the day Mama drew the pattern on the burlap and attached it to the frame, and that helped. She would work on the rug some evenings when all the housework was done, saying that she should have drawn something simpler. This rug would never be finished, she insisted.

Yes, it will, Mama, I promised, and I set to work.

Le 20 février 1885

Emma had never heard of the sort of winter fishing that is carried on by Métis until she and her family came here. At Toronto they sometimes drill holes through the ice and then fish with a line. Unlike us, though, they do not use a wooden jigger to pull a net from one hole, then under the ice, and then out again through a second hole. It must take the people in Toronto a very long time to catch enough fish to feed a large family. Perhaps they eat less.

Papa and Moushoom checked our fish nets, as they do every few days. Yesterday they caught something of interest. By the time Armand had come running, shouting that Louise and I must see the beast, it lay gutted in the snow, surrounded by admiring men and boys. The beast was a sturgeon, a huge creature full of eggs which Papa carefully removed as he cleaned the fish.

Armand claimed the sturgeon's bony head with its chin whiskers, but when he picked it up he slipped on the bloody ice and the head flew out of his hands. He and the boys began to kick this dreadful prize back and forth across the ice, seeing who could make it slide the farthest. How Louise laughed! She said it looked like a game they play up in Prince Albert. Curling, she said it was called. When she explained how it was played, the boys ran home and returned in minutes armed with brooms.

I claimed the intestines for the barn cats and had to make two trips with my pail filled, while Louise made two trips to carry in the eggs. That night for supper we ate some of the sturgeon and eggs fried in bacon grease. They were delicious, and since the cats' pan was quickly emptied, they must have thought the same about the intestines.

Louise says that there are people who cure sturgeon eggs with salt and sell them for a great deal of money. I would rather eat the eggs just the way I did tonight. As for the sturgeon-head game, the curling, it makes me wonder about men who play at such things.

Le 21 février 1885

There are now four small dogs on the back wall of the cabin. They are chasing what looks a bit like a sturgeon. I suppose I should say something to Armand, but it is more interesting to wait and see what will happen.

Plus tard

Papa says there will be a community meeting at St. Antoine church.

Le 22 février 1885

There will be no music or singing until Lent is over and *Zhour di Pawk* is here. The house seems oddly quiet without the sound of Papa's fiddle. It is a sacrifice we must make, though, and his music will seem even sweeter once we may again enjoy it.

Papa made his own fiddle out of birchbark and maple wood when he was a young man. Emma's mother plays the fiddle, but she did not make hers. Her husband bought it for her. And it is a violin, Madame MacLeod has told me, not a fiddle, a valuable instrument called a Villaume that came from Ottawa.

I heard her play that violin once. It did not sound at all like any Métis fiddle I have ever heard, even though it looks somewhat like one. They say that names have a certain power. It must be true, because that Ottawa violin sounded so sad, a person could have cried to hear it. Poor unhappy Villaume.

Somehow this all makes me think of the conversation I had with Emma, the one about the word half-breed. I am Métis, but if I were a fiddle I would not be a Villaume, I would be a *vyloōn* like Papa.

Le 23 février 1885

People are talking about William Jackson, Monsieur Riel's secretary. They say he is taking instruction from Père Moulin, and that Monsieur Jackson wishes to be baptized. How wonderful!

Le 24 février 1885

Only the men went to the meeting at the church. Louise and I remained home with Armand, she with her knitting and I with my hooking. When Papa and the others came home, I could not believe the news. Monsieur Riel said that he planned to leave Batoche! He fears his presence here will only be harmful to the Métis cause.

What an uproar this created, Moushoom said. The men shouted out in protest. They refused to lose their leader. Even Père Fourmond agreed and blessed Monsieur Riel.

They say he will stay. That the North-West Mounted Police might come from Fort Carlton, as some people fear, does not matter. I suppose I must trust in the judgement of my father and the other men, but the thought of police here is so very frightening. I have heard the stories about what happens when the police come. Enough, though, or I will never sleep.

Le 25 février 1885

Last night snow fell. There was no wind and so it came straight down. When I looked out my window, the yard was smooth and white except for the small marks of birds, and the footprints and tail markings of mice.

There was also something else. Papa said that someone's ox must have escaped from a barn, and that the fool — he was speaking about the owner, not the ox — did not deserve to own an ox if that was how he kept it. Armand whispered to me that maybe the *roogaroo* had come around, or maybe *googoosh,* although he was not certain exactly how their feet looked. I was sure that Moushoom would laugh, but he did not.

I walked out with Moushoom. He was quiet for a long while, examining the tracks, smelling the air, not even looking at the windows where everyone was watching. He told me to study the tracks, to remember how they looked. "It is the most important thing you will ever see," he whispered. I said to myself that the footprints of any ox could not be that important.

"Not an ox," said Moushoom. He can read my mind. "A buffalo made this, Josephine. What sort of Métis will you be when we go on the hunt, if you cannot see even that small thing, my girl?"

Later Papa said that he sometimes worries about Moushoom and the way he lives in the past. It has been so many years since the buffalo ran here. Living in the past is the troubling thing about growing old, Papa said.

I worry too.

Avant de dormir

Now the dogs and sturgeon have been joined by a buffalo and what I think is a boy. It is hard to tell, though, as the boy has no body, only a head with sticks growing out of it, sticks that end in chicken feet.

Le 26 février 1885

Seeing those tracks in the snow yesterday made Moushoom think about buffalo. It also made him tell stories about the hunts. Fortunately, he did not ask me to write them all down, for they would have filled this whole book.

"Only one," he said. "This one, and get it right, you girl who cannot recognize a buffalo's tracks. This is about the 1840 buffalo hunt, the best one I can remember."

Here are his words:

The Buffalo Hunt of 1840
Told by Moushoom Bouvier

More than a thousand carts with more than a thousand men and their women left that *juin.* Hard to count the children because they wiggled so, but there were hundreds. Gabriel Dumont was there with his parents, just a small boy, but I could already imagine what a hunter he would become. He had the look even then. There were hundreds of carthorses, oxen and buffalo runners. Best horse in the world, a buffalo runner. Nothing can scare it.

We went more than two hundred miles in less than twenty days, and then there was the herd. Josephine, it was a blanket of buffalo covering the prairie, offering itself to us the way the animals used to. The priest said Mass that morning. Even I attended, for when you set out for buffalo you need all the blessings you can get.

We followed the Laws of the Hunt, and they were as important as the Commandments. Break a law once and your saddle and bridle would be cut up. A second offence and your coat would be cut up. And for a third offence, you were flogged. A thief would be shamed publicly. There was no hunting on Sunday. All of us rode together unless we had permission to do otherwise, and no one began before the order was given. I was a captain of the hunt that year, and so was Gabriel's papa Isadore. I tell you, I was stricter than the St. Laurent nuns!

Later someone told me that at least thirteen hundred buffalo were killed that first day. When it was all over, my share was a couple of thousand pounds of pemmican in the three carts my first wife and I had brought with us. That was a good hunt. I fed my family that winter, and the men at the Hudson's Bay Company paid me well for the pemmican I later sold to them. Many years of good hunts and many bags of money. Shillings, French coins, American dollars. Never had all that much use for money, though, except for what it bought for the family, and I did not need much money for that, only a little sugar and some flour. I would trade a pot of money today, though, for just one pot of buffalo marrow.

I think about those buffalo now and again. Not the ones that ran and lived, or even the ones we killed. I think about what we left behind. All those skinned and gutted bodies, all the meat we did not use but left for the wolves, coyotes and ravens. All those bones. Mountains of bones. Sometimes I wonder if the bones are why the buffalo no longer offer themselves to us. Maybe if we had picked them up right away instead of leaving them there. Mostly though, I just remember the hunt and what fine good days those were.

"Take a lesson from that, Josephine."

I told him that I would, but now I am not sure just what lesson I should take.

Le 27 février 1885

Tonight we

Plus tard

My fingers were so chilled I could not hold the pen. So I have begun again.

Tonight we stood outside for a long while and watched the sky. The stars were there, and so was the moon, but there was more. The blackness of the night sky was alive with the *chirāān* — how I love those beautiful lights when they come out. They were dancing across the north, and so Papa said there would be a cold north wind the next day.

Armand began to whistle, but then stopped when Moushoom reminded him that whistling could bring down the spirits of the dead, for that is what the lights are. Armand replied that Père Moulin says they are just lights, and that lights cannot decide the wind's direction. Moushoom made a snorting sound, and said that the priest had no proof at all for those words. Who was Père Moulin to make such rash statements?

As for me, I only know that Mama is a spirit now,

and that she is in Heaven. When I saw the *chirāān*, I only saw something beautiful.

Le 28 février 1885

A very cold wind today, but then it is winter and cold winds are to be expected. Moushoom went outside, wet his finger and held it up. "North," was all that he said.

Plus tard

During supper tonight, Moushoom said that someone has been drawing strange pictures on his cabin. Dogs and a large fish and some sort of unpleasant-looking monster. Then he said that if he caught that someone, the person would be very sorry. A wise person would rub out the pictures. Soon.

Armand was strangely quiet for the rest of the meal.

Le 1 mars 1885

Adrian heard that Monsieur Riel spoke to the congregation on the steps of St. Laurent de Grandin church this morning. "What did he say?" I asked. "Was it another declaration to the Sacred Heart of Jesus?"

It was not. Monsieur Riel said that it is time for the Métis people to bare their teeth. Armand laughed and laughed at these words and made savage noises. "I am a Métis *roogaroo,"* he growled, and Eagle growled with him. "See my fierce teeth! If Macdonald or his followers come here, I will bite them and save you, Josephine and Louise."

A year ago, the thought of me needing to be saved would have been amusing. Now it is not.

Le 2 mars 1885

This morning Edmond told us that Moushoom's hands and knees were painful with the aching that bothers them from time to time. Moushoom would take supper later in his cabin rather than coming up to the big house. I decided to ride over to Nohkom LaBute's farm. Burdock tea is what he needs, she said. And she should know, for she is *la septième,* the seventh daughter born to her parents, and so she has the power of healing.

Then, in the afternoon, Armand and I walked down to the cabin, my brother carrying a pot of stew while I carried a kettle of burdock tea. I had made sure the meat in that stew was soft and well cooked, since Moushoom has no teeth.

There he was, his aching knees and hands wrapped in muskrat skins that also soothe pain. He hugged

Armand, who ran off to explore the hollows that are tucked under the riverbank. One of the hollows is surrounded by the roots of a large tree, and Armand has dug and deepened it into a cave until it is almost like a small root-lined room. Armand calls it Fort Bouvier. There is a Fort Carlton on the other side of the river beyond Duck Lake, after all. Why not a Fort Bouvier? This always makes Moushoom smile, because although Armand may say he is making a fort, in truth he is looking for the *Ma-ma-kwa-se-sak*.

Moushoom thinks that Armand will never see the little people who live in the caves — he makes too much noise when he plays there. Besides, the little people are hardly ever seen these days, even when a gift of candy is left. Too much disturbance, too much uproar.

Emma calls the little people fairies, but she does not believe they exist. I myself have never seen even one of the *Ma-ma-kwa-se-sak,* but I have not seen the ocean either. I believe it is there, though. They say that if you see one of the little people you will have good luck. We could use some of that.

Plus tard

Looking for the *Ma-ma-kwa-se-sak* was not all Armand did this afternoon. All the drawings are now gone from Moushoom's cabin wall.

Le 3 mars 1885

A robin landed on the windowsill for a moment today. It is early for him to have returned, but still it cheered me. Mama used to say that a person should take comfort in small and ordinary things. I do.

Plus tard

Armand is small, but certainly not ordinary, for he has been teaching the chickens. That they wander about pecking in the yard does not bother him at all. He makes his voice deep — I suppose he thinks he sounds like Père Moulin — and orders them to say the alphabet or count to ten. When the rooster crowed today, Armand was convinced that the bird understood him.

It seems so long ago that I played like that.

Avant de dormir

It is hard to find ways to take our minds away from the troubles with the government, and what is worse, Papa and Adrian have argued. It seems to me that more and more our lives are being poisoned by all this. Only here will I admit how worried I am not only for Batoche but for our family. When Mama was alive, no one —

No. I will not think that thought again.

So. Tonight I read a story to Armand, one from Louise's book. He has been asking for this story for some time, since it is more or less about the *Ma-ma-kwa-se-sak*. Monsieur Perrault has titled it "Les Fées."

In the story, the little people test two girls. Jewels and gold fall from the mouth of the good girl and she marries the king's son. As for the bad girl, snakes and toads fall from her mouth and she comes to an unhappy ending.

The moral was a suitable one. It said that diamonds and gold coins may work some wonders in their way, but a gentle word is worth more than all the gems on earth. Armand said that a mouthful of toads and snakes would be more fun. I believe the moral was wasted on him, but still, it made me smile inside.

Le 4 mars 1885

This morning Papa was taken by curiosity to see how Gabriel Dumont's new house is coming along. He and Adrian were gone most of the day, and have only just arrived home a few hours ago. I must admit I was a little worried. Batoche no longer feels as safe as it once did, but my father and brother are capable men.

As for the building, it is not yet finished and so it seems that Madame Dumont and the washing machine will have to wait for their fine house.

To bed, Josephine.

Le 5 mars 1885

We spent a quiet day at home, with no worrisome talk. Edmond and Moushoom played cards. Papa and Adrian did not. Instead, they cleaned their guns and sharpened all the knives in the house, since they have given up cards for Lent. Louise and I saw to supper, making a *rababoo* of fish and vegetables. She used her own recipe, and so the food tasted different, but everyone seemed to enjoy it.

Armand played string games — cat's cradle, Emma calls this — but they could not hold his attention for long, and he began to tease the puppy until Eagle nipped him.

"Enough!" shouted Moushoom. He does not shout often and so Armand's chin began to tremble. Armand looked to Papa for sympathy, but he only shrugged. "What Armand needs . . . " Moushoom went on, but then he paused. I supposed he wanted to give Armand time to think about what he needed. Finally, my grandfather said that Armand needed to help him with the *cariole.* He added that I should help as well. Neither Armand nor I should spend so much time indoors, especially on a fine day such as this.

Moushoom's *cariole* is beautiful, the birch runners smooth and slick when they travel over the snow. It is old, but the buffalo-hide panels on its sides are kept brightly painted. The harnesses are not ordinary leather, either. They are *shaganappi* that Moushoom braided himself, since buffalo hide is far stronger. All three of his dogs pull the *cariole,* but Moon is always the lead dog. He also wears the finest *tapis* — and actually seems proud to wear a coat all trimmed with bells and ribbons, if a dog can be said to look proud.

Leaving Eagle behind in the warm house, Armand and I dressed the dogs while Moushoom pulled the *cariole* out of the shed near his cabin. When all was ready, when the dogs were in their harnesses, when Armand and I were seated in the *cariole,* Moushoom threw a buffalo robe over our laps. He whistled to the dogs, cracked his whip over their heads — the whip never touches his dogs — and we were off. *Pimbahtaw!* he shouted, and they took us along the river past the Caron house and the Gareau house. There was the cemetery and there was the church, both looking peaceful under the snow. We flew into Batoche and Moushoom slowed down the dogs so that we could wave and call out to anyone who happened to be looking. They might wish to admire us, after all. Then out we flew again.

Moushoom and the dogs took us all the way to

St. Laurent. We passed the old schoolhouse where Monsieur Riel and his family are now living. In front of it were three balls of snow that his children had rolled and put into a pile. The figure leaned a bit to one side. It was beginning to melt in the sun, I suppose.

After we returned home, Armand described every moment. When Papa put him to bed, I heard him saying that tomorrow he, Armand, was going to make a man out of snow for our house, just like Jean-Louis Riel's.

Papa says the Riels have almost nothing. The stove they use has been borrowed. They have no beds and so must sleep on the floor. Save for the generosity of the nuns there at St. Laurent, the Riel children would be going without milk. Louis Riel is a proud man, Papa said, but perhaps he would accept some fish for the sake of his little ones. My father is so kind.

Plus tard

Louise mended shirts after we said the rosary. I must admit her stitches are very close and even.

Le 6 mars 1885

Papa and Adrian left the house to take fish to the Riels. I would have liked to go along, but Papa

Plus tard

Louise and I had company that arrived just as I began to write, earlier. Several of our neighbours, Madame Chene and her daughter Agathe, Madame Jacob, who is Louise's cousin, and Nohkom LaBute came to visit. So had two of Papa's sisters, *ma tawnt* Bernice and *ma tawnt* Solange. All brought sewing, knitting or finger weaving with them, since even when we are visiting we keep our hands busy. What chattering there was!

It was Nohkom LaBute who brought the news. Nothing stays hidden for long here at Batoche, and even less stays hidden from *her.* It had taken only a short while for her to learn that a secret meeting had been held at Gabriel's Crossing yesterday. She named some of the men who had attended. Ten of them had signed an oath that Monsieur Riel had written, she told us. They marked their *X*s and pledged to live holy lives in all respects.

Later, when our visitors had gone, when supper was done and Armand in bed, Papa told us that Nohkom LaBute did not know everything about that meeting. When he and Adrian had been at the Riels' earlier today, a group of men had arrived to further discuss certain serious matters. It seemed that Monsieur Nolin had also been asked to sign the oath. He had refused, saying that first we should have nine days of prayer to examine our consciences. When asked his opinion, Papa had agreed. Proceeding with caution and a clear conscience was wise.

As for the oath, Papa told us there was a second part to it. In signing, the men vowed to save our country from the wicked government, even if it meant taking up arms. "I will fight to protect what is mine," he said. "And I do not need to put my *X* on anything to prove I have the resolve. I am a man of peace, though, as I have said many times."

Taking up arms against the government would be a risky undertaking, Papa went on, a desperate one. If war came, he prayed it would come only after every last effort had been made to reason with the government.

"What can you do but take action when you stand to lose everything?" Adrian asked him. "When evil shows its face, a man must resist." Then Adrian said that even if he had not signed the oath, he had signed it in spirit.

Papa was silent for a very long time, as if he was trying to decide what to say and what not to say. Then he told us that he had seen a man executed once. It was at Upper Fort Garry during the Red River troubles. I have never seen his face so grim. He told us exactly what had happened to a man whose name was Thomas Scott, but I will not write such a terrible thing here, only that the man suffered greatly and did not die quickly. When Papa said that he hoped he would not live to see anything like that again, and that he prayed none of us would either, I knew he was telling the truth.

Now I sit in my bed writing this. I can hear Papa, Adrian and Moushoom talking in the kitchen. Moushoom had his say. "To us it would be a resistance," he told Papa and Adrian, "But Macdonald and his kind will see it as a rebellion. And they will have another word for it. They will call it treason." The very word makes me shiver. I know what the government would do to a traitor.

So. There is to be a special novena that will begin next Tuesday, and end on the feast day of our Métis patron St. Joseph. Surely all those days of prayer will bring wisdom. Now, though, I am no longer trying to make out the words coming from the kitchen. I have no desire to, not after Papa described exactly what happened to that man who died at Fort Garry.

Tard

I have had a horrible dream, one that I cannot put out of my mind. In it, I am there at the fort in Red River instead of Papa. Thomas Scott kneels in the snow waiting for the firing squad to execute him. I know, the way you know in dreams, that Monsieur

Riel does not want Scott to die. It is what the people want, though, and besides, Scott hates the Métis and all that we stand for. Still, I try to tell Monsieur Riel that Scott must not die, that if he does, Macdonald and the people of Ontario will never forgive him. No words come from my mouth, though. I am unable to speak. The rifles fire, but Thomas Scott does not die immediately, even when one of the men shoots him in the head. Finally, they put him into his casket, but I can hear him calling me, calling that I should join him.

That is when I woke.

Papa is right. No one should ever have to see such things, and yet war is coming. What will I see then?

Le 8 mars 1885

Papa and our men went to the church at St. Laurent today for yet another meeting. The news was not good, Papa told us when they returned. "There is little chance that we will get title to our land, and there are some who may even lose their farms," he said. "How will we live? For years there have been no buffalo, and there are fewer and fewer jobs freighting. Some people have stores or businesses, but only the land stands between my family and starvation." And he put his arm around Louise.

When Adrian suggested that perhaps I should

take Armand upstairs, Moushoom said no. "They need to hear this," he said, "especially Josephine. How can she write this story if she does not know all of it?"

Armand paid little attention, preferring to draw pictures on his slate. I, though, sat and listened to every word. Monsieur Riel has decided we will have our own government, since Ottawa is deaf to the Métis' pleas. It will be a provisional government, he told everyone — provisional means temporary, Louise explained — and it will be dissolved once Macdonald comes to his senses. Gabriel Dumont said that messengers must be sent to One Arrow and to all the other chiefs. We needed their support, and needed it badly.

They talked for hours. Papa finally carried Armand to bed. Louise banked the fire in the stove and bid me goodnight. Adrian left the kitchen yawning mightily, and then Moushoom and Edmond slipped away to their cabin. It was so peaceful just then, with all talk of governments and fighting ended.

Plus tard

I must put this down here before I forget. A reporter who writes stories for a newspaper was at that meeting. He came all the way from Toronto just to write about what is happening here. How strange to think that in a few days people in Toronto will be reading about Batoche and all of us.

Plus tard

I said nothing to Louise when she bid me good-night. It felt good to ignore her, especially after Papa put

I will not write that.

Moushoom says that feelings can sweeten life or sour it beyond belief. All I feel at this moment is shame.

Le 9 mars 1885

Marie-Antoinette sounded just after dawn today. Nine peals rang out and so we knew that a man had passed on. Later we learned that it was not a man, but a newborn boy, the child of one of Nohkom LaBute's daughters who lives near Prince Albert. Her poor little *bābee* lived only a few hours.

Sometimes life is hard, but still it is precious. How sad to die before you begin your life's journey.

Plus tard

Louise and I took a pot of *rababoo* over to Nohkom's house this afternoon. The *bābee's* death had saddened her, but she was at peace, saying that one must accept God's will.

Louise was very quiet as we walked home. Finally, to my surprise, she said that she was not sure which was more difficult, losing a loved one or accepting the will of God. I was not certain either, since both can be so difficult, which was what I said to her. Louise smiled a little, but it was a sad sort of smile.

I cannot stop seeing that smile, and the sadness in it. Louise has feelings, of course, but she does not make a show of them. Mama was like that as well. She always said that women, especially wives, are the glue that holds a family together. It is their job to make the home a peaceful place, no matter what the cost to themselves.

Louise. I suppose it is a hard thing she has taken on.

Le 10 mars 1885

The novena began today. Père Fourmond said Mass and Père Moulin assisted him. The church at St. Laurent was very crowded, and I could not see Monsieur Riel among the faces. Neither could anyone else in our family. Odd.

Le 11 mars 1885

A rainy day, but that did not stop people from attending the novena. Perhaps Madame Riel's cough has worsened, for she and her family were again absent.

Le 12 mars 1885

The novena's sermons are strange, and it seems to me that they have little to do with our souls or consciences. Père Fourmond insists that we must obey the priests, which is nothing new. But now he also insists we must obey the government.

When Papa repeated this, Moushoom threw up his hands and I could tell that a particularly rude word was ready to come out. Because Louise and I were present, he contented himself with, "*Abain,* since when do Métis obey their oppressors?"

Le 13 mars 1885

There were a good many sucker fish in the traps today. Papa and Moushoom plan to smoke the carcasses, but Louise and I boiled the heads for supper. I always enjoy the heads. I also enjoy waiting to see how long it will take Moushoom to say something about the bones.

"Of course, they have all those bones," Moushoom began finally, although no one had said a word about them. This was at the end of the meal when I thought that perhaps, just this once, he would not tell the sucker story. Moushoom heard the story from his grandmother, who was very fond of stick gambling. She had heard it from a cousin who once spent two winters among people who lived by the western ocean. In the cousin's story, one day a sucker fish made a bet with an eel. All either of them had to bet was their bones. Guess who won? It is why the sucker fish has so many bones and the eel is boneless.

The sucker's head is a strange-looking thing, filled with a puzzle of tiny bones. People say that each of these bones is shaped like one of the animals found in the bush. I cannot see this myself, but Armand says he can. He especially likes the mouth bones, which Papa says look like caribou antlers. Not ever having seen a caribou, I cannot be certain.

After supper, Louise gave Armand an old ledger that came from her father-in-law's house, telling him that the remaining blank pages would be perfect for drawing pictures. He was so pleased! It was a happy day.

Plus tard

I cannot stop thinking about that ledger. Or about Louise. I would very much like to ask her a certain question about what she knows about certain drawings, but perhaps not asking is better. Mama used to say that a little mystery in life is a good thing. I agree.

Le 14 mars 1885

Today I helped Louise take out some of the rugs. We hung them on the line and beat the dust out of them. As we did this, lines of geese flew over us. They seemed so free, and all I could think of was that no one oppresses them. I suppose they may be killed by men, but none landed, and they flew too high for anyone to shoot them. Clever geese!

Plus tard

A letter from Louise's sister Rose arrived a few hours ago. In it, Madame Montour told her about a wondrous thing that would be happening. It is an *éclipse,* and it seems that the moon's shadow will cover the sun. Louise explained it to us, but even with the drawings she made in Armand's ledger, it was difficult to believe. It is she who told me the spelling of the word, I should add. Louise spells very well. She also warned that we must not look directly at this *éclipse,* for the sun could burn our eyes. We could be blinded. Papa is to smoke a piece of glass for us to look through.

Moushoom says that he will have to see this to believe it. Only through the glass, though, he added.

Le 15 mars 1885

Monsieur Riel was at the novena this morning, along with his ten followers who have declared themselves our government. All was peaceful until Père Fourmond said that the priests would refuse the sacraments to anyone who took up arms in revolt. No confession, no communion. Nothing at all. How it made me shiver! To die without the benefit of the sacraments would mean going straight to Hell. But then Monsieur Riel stood up and began to scold Père Fourmond. How dare he refuse the sacraments to people who would be defending their sacred rights! Père Fourmond said nothing more.

When Papa told Moushoom this, he laughed, and said perhaps he would start to go back to church if it was going to be so entertaining.

Le 16 mars 1885

Today the shadow of the moon covered the sun almost completely. Papa had smoked a piece of a broken pane by holding it over the chimney of a lit lamp, until the glass was covered in soot. When the moon's shadow began to cover the sun — this was around noon — we went out into the yard and took turns watching the spectacle.

It was so beautiful, almost the colour of a rose.

And the air! It was a cold day, but when the sun was hidden, it became colder than ever. I have never thought to see or feel such things.

Le 17 mars 1885

So this is what they in the east think of us.

RIPE FOR A REBELLION.

LOUIS RIEL ONCE MORE ADVISING A REVOLT.

Half-breeds of the Northwest Territories Greatly Excited — Developments Anxiously Awaited.

SASKATCHEWAN, N.W.T., March 12. —

The half-breeds population here is on the verge of a rebellion. Secret meetings are frequently held and ominous threats are indulged in. On Sunday last Louis Riel addressed a large gathering outside the church at Batoche, telling them that war between England and Russia was imminent, and this was the time for them to strike a blow for their rights. Developments are awaited with some apprehension. It is said

> Riel is working with a large body of Fenians in Minnesota and Montana, who promise to make a raid on Canadian territory simultaneously with the half-breed rising. It is urged that England will be unable to spare any troops to suppress the rebellion and that at the best Canada's citizen forces with the military schools and mounted police thrown in will not be any better skilled in warfare than the untrained hosts that can be thrown against them.

Papa said that he remembered hearing about these Fenians back when our family still lived at the old Red River settlement. They were Irishmen, if he was not mistaken, and came from a place not so far from where Moushoom's stove had been made. Back then, the Fenians had called upon Louis Riel to support their cause, which was freeing themselves from the slavery of the English. Papa never could understand how they thought invading Canada could do that.

When Armand asked whether the Fenian slaves were coming to see Monsieur Riel, Papa and Louise looked at each other while biting their lips. This was probably wise, as Armand does not care to be laughed at. Who does?

It was hard to explain, Papa told him, adding that he did not think the Fenians would come. Louise, though, drew an amazing picture for Armand in his ledger. Here was Canada and the North-West Territory, and this was the Saskatchewan River with Batoche on its bank. She marked Duck Lake, Prince Albert, Gabriel's Crossing, Tourond's Coulee, and all the places around here. This was our farm, and the church and the forge. Here was the Fenians' homeland, all the way across the ocean. Ireland it was called. And here was Scotland where Moushoom's stove had been made.

Armand added to the picture, drawing our goats, dogs — including little Eagle — cats and the stove. He even drew *googoosh* hiding under a bed with a *roogaroo* sitting on it. "That will keep them away," he said proudly. "The soldiers too! They will not dare to come here!"

I wish it were so.

Plus tard

I cannot help but think of Papa and Louise, and the way they looked at each other. I could see happiness and closeness in that look. It is hard for me to write this, but it made me happy too. Perhaps that is not such a bad thing.

Très tard

It has taken me all day to compose myself and to compose the words I wish to write. It seems —

Calmly, Josephine. It seems to me that what I write here is important.

The fight with the government's men has begun. News came to us in bits, stirring everyone up. First we heard that the police were coming to arrest Monsieur Riel, and that was when our men began to act. Papa, Edmond and Moushoom went with other men to Clarke's Crossing, and cut the telegraph lines to keep the police from sending any messages. It gave us all heart that they could not call for reinforcements.

So much happened! Gabriel Dumont brought in prisoners — John Lash the Indian agent and William Tompkins, who is his interpreter, had the misfortune to run into Monsieur Dumont on their way back from One Arrow. Some of our men went into the Kerr brothers' store and seized the guns, ammunition and many other things from it.

And our church! St. Antoine is now a *headquarters* rather than a simple place of worship. We all went there to join the great crowd who were squeezed inside. Monsieur Riel spoke to us. At first he wanted to leave, saying that we would be more easily able to get what we wanted if he was not here.

But the people would not have this.

Papa says we must be strong, because God will protect and aid those who are in the right.

I will try, but so much is tumbling around inside me. I am afraid. Who would not be? Yet I am excited, but it is a strange sort of excitement, almost like the way I feel just before a bad thunderstorm.

I cannot stop thinking about the church. My brothers and I were baptized there. Mama's funeral Mass was said within the church's walls. The church belongs to all of us here at Batoche, but somehow it always has seemed to me that most of all it belongs to St. Antoine himself. Père Moulin once told us that St. Antoine was a great speaker, and that everywhere he went people came to listen. Just like Monsieur Riel.

I know that St. Antoine watches over the church. The thought of him doing that comforts me, but I also take comfort in the fact that Monsieur Riel is still with us.

Le 18 mars 1885

There is such an odd feeling here. Not in the house, but in Batoche itself.

Moushoom says it is almost the same as what he felt each time he rode out in the buffalo hunt. You never knew what would happen, but you rode out anyway, because that is what a man did.

Edmond thinks that Batoche has never been so united. Last night when Monsieur Riel spoke to the crowd, he told me, people shouted that if they had to die for their country, they would all die together. Edmond agreed completely.

I cannot

Plus tard

Tears. I am not a crier, but so many tears these days. I cannot bear to think of the men I love dying in battle. Papa, Adrian, Moushoom. What would life be like with even one of them gone? And yes, Edmond. I care for him as well, although only here can I say that. He is a good friend, but he is far more than a friend.

Le 19 mars 1885

Today was the last day of the novena and the feast of St. Joseph. It was also the day on which William Jackson was baptized, taking the name of Honoré Joseph Jaxon. Men saluted him by firing their guns into the air. As I heard the gunshots, my mind went back to the first hours of January when Papa fired his own rifle to welcome in the new year. I had no idea then what sort of year this one would be.

Papa says a council has been formed, one that

people are calling *le petit provisoire* since Monsieur Riel's name for it is so difficult to say. Adrian has told me, but it is a word I could not even begin to spell. The council is made up of seventeen Métis men, a *Kanayah* and a Dakota Sioux chief named White Cap. Monsieur Riel is not a member, which I cannot understand, but to Adrian it makes perfect sense. Monsieur Riel says that he prefers to be one of the flock, Adrian told us, that he is no more than we are. Then Adrian said that Gabriel Dumont is now the general of our army.

"Army?" asked Louise. "But we are so few. Hardly an army. Surely Macdonald will send hundreds and hundreds against us."

Her words made me feel cold inside, because I could hear the truth in them.

Papa told us that we should try not to worry. Even Monsieur Riel does not expect there would be any actual fighting, since all this fuss is simply to get the attention of the government. On the other hand, it would be best if Armand stayed away from school and remained at home. That much wisdom, at least, Papa felt he had gained from the novena. Armand screamed with joy until Louise said he would continue his lessons with her and me.

How can I not worry?

Le 22 mars 1885

The talk outside the church after Mass this morning was only of war. They say five hundred soldiers are on their way to Batoche. Five hundred men whose lives are about nothing but the business of killing. I cannot imagine such men.

Tard

I hoped that I would sleep through the night. I was wrong. When I woke, I could see the moon through my window. It was a perfect half moon, and so very white. It was sad somehow. After all, they say that the moon and the sun cannot see each other from across the sky — only now and again is it possible. It is only something that people say, but still, can the moon see what is going to happen here? Will the sun watch those soldiers coming closer and closer?

It is just a story, but I am so afraid. And it is so hard not to let it show.

Le 23 mars 1885

This morning when Moushoom and Edmond came to the house, Edmond said he has heard that Emma's mother wants to go back to Ontario. She misses her family. I said that I hoped this would not happen, as the MacLeods are part of their community. They are also our friends. Moushoom said he has been thinking about people who are not Métis like we are. One must remember that it is possible that the English half-breeds and the *Kanayaens* wish us well, but had they not just voted yesterday that they would not fight? For people like them the law is always more important than matters of friendship.

Papa thinks that maybe the MacLeods feel the same way. They come from Toronto, after all. They are English whites and perhaps their opinions are the same as those of the English half-breeds. There is also the unfortunate fact that Emma's father has had no luck at all with his farming. His animals have died, his ploughshare has broken again and again, and of course his wife longs for her family. It seems to me that it must be hard being so far from one's family. Adrian said that maybe he would ask them himself when he went over to visit Emma later.

I myself have not seen Emma in a long while. Only her papa comes to Batoche these days. How sad. Finally I decided what to do. Adrian agreed to help. Even now, Emma will be reading the letter he carried to her. I will copy it here.

Dear Emma,

We are faced with hard times and I cannot say what will come of them.

No matter what happens, I remain your friend.

Josephine Bouvier

Le soir

I have no idea what Emma thought of my letter. She did not write a reply for Adrian to bring back. He said nothing at first, and it hurt me to see how hard he was fighting to keep himself from tears. I understood the reason, given what he told us once he had brought his emotions under control.

Emma's mother will no longer permit Adrian to see her, and Emma will not be allowed to visit here any more. Her father spoke to Adrian outside the house. Adrian is to take no offense, he said — none of us should — but with the Métis' position regarding the business with Riel, his wife is frightened. What could he do? His wife's peace of mind and their daughter's safety come first, and so his family must side with the other English settlers.

Papa shook his head but said that Emma must obey her parents. And we would take no offence. There would be no point in it.

"Zhi bustee koum un kloo," said Adrian in his misery. His shoulders slumped, and how it hurt me to

see him almost broken, the way a nail is when it is bent.

I feel the same way, but I will not despair. I do not think, though, that the closer friendship I might have had with Emma can survive these events.

Le 25 mars 1885

Monsieur Riel has started his own church, something that Papa says troubles Père Moulin greatly. There is now a chapel here at Batoche, one that he has made in a room on the second floor of Monsieur Boyer's house. Some people go there to pray. Papa has forbidden us to pray there — not that I would think to do that in such a place — but he did not forbid me to look at it. And so today when I walked over to Monsieur Letendre's store to buy liniment, I did just that.

At one end of the room, there is a large picture of Our Lady of Lourdes with St. Bernadette praying at her feet. A figure of Christ hangs above it. Several men were praying the rosary while three girls sang a hymn.

I cannot understand what is happening here. It is almost as though Batoche has been turned upside down and inside out until all the familiar things are gone.

Le 26 mars 1885

A terrible day. I must write slowly, and be strong.

So. Papa and our men left this morning with Moushoom's *cariole* to check their muskrat traps up and across the river. Some time later, around ten o'clock, as Armand sat at the table struggling with a lesson and Louise and I had nearly finished scrubbing the kitchen floor, we heard distant gunfire. Had our men seen ducks or geese on the river? Again and again, shots rang out. It soon became clear that it was not the sound of hunting.

Both Louise and I tossed our brushes into the bucket and went to stand outside, Armand next to me. I cannot say whether Louise reached out or whether I did, but our hands clasped. Finally we all went inside and shut the door, but we could not shut out the sound of the gunfire. For almost one half hour it went on, and then there was silence.

The brushes remained in the bucket. Armand no longer worked at his lesson. We waited, and waited even more. Never has time passed so slowly for me. The hands of the clock seemed almost to be frozen to its face.

"They must have stopped somewhere to visit," I said to Louise.

"Perhaps they took time for a game of billiards," she answered.

"Yes," cried Armand, "a game of billiards!"

Suddenly we heard the sound of the dogs' bells. Armand went back to his lesson, Louise turned to the stove, I picked a scrub brush out of the bucket, and then the kitchen was filled with Papa, Edmond, Adrian and Moushoom. The trapping was successful, we were told. There were a dozen fat muskrats for us to gut and skin, and two plump mallards as well.

I should have felt the weight of fear lifting from my heart as I worked with Louise, but I did not. So many shots fired for just two ducks?

We skinned the muskrats and cleaned them, carefully removing the musk glands so that the meat would not be tainted. Moushoom will tan the skins and keep a few of them to soothe his hands. The rest of the pelts he will bring over to Letendre's for trade. And, of course, he will take a few of the muskrat carcasses over to One Arrow tomorrow.

We boiled the muskrats and put them in the oven to roast. Then we feasted.

Muskrat flesh cleanses your insides, and since spring is the time for cleansing, it is a good food for this time of year. They were delicious, and as I ate, I was sure I could feel myself beginning to be cleansed of worry and doubt.

Then when supper was cleared away and the dishes washed, Papa told us what had happened, what the gunshots had meant. There had been a battle at Duck Lake. Nearly three hundred Métis, and our Cree allies, against maybe one hundred of the North-West Mounted Police from Fort Carlton and their volunteers from Prince Albert. My heart began to pound at the thought of those men having been so close to us. When the fighting began, Papa and our men were nearly ready to cross the river and head for home. Word came to them that reinforcements were needed. Of course, they went to the aid of Dumont and the army.

He sighed, and with that sigh, my hands grew damp, because I knew something worse was coming.

Finally Papa spoke again. Gabriel Dumont was wounded, and badly enough, but his brother Isadore and three others of our Métis men — Jean-Baptiste Montour, August Laframboise and Joseph Montour — are dead.

The police had also killed a Cree ally named Assiyiwin. Twelve of the enemy were dead. At all this news, my stomach turned into a hard knot, and the muskrat I had eaten threatened to come up. All I could see in my head were scenes of the revenge that would surely now threaten us.

When I asked about Monsieur Riel, Papa answered that he had not fought. Instead he sat on his horse, a crucifix in his hand, and prayed for the brave Métis fighters.

Armand cried out in excitement that it had worked, that we had won, and Papa opened his mouth to say something, but then he paused. Finally he told Armand to ready himself for bed.

Duck Lake. When I pray tonight, it will be in hope that Emma and her family are unhurt. I will give thanks that Papa and the men of our family are unharmed. They could have been killed, their bodies still out there in the darkness and the cold. Just the thought of it

Plus tard

Edmond came back to the house earlier. Moushoom needed some rat root and there was none in the cabin. His throat was sore from shouting out war whoops during the battle, Edmond told me.

I took the rat root out to Moushoom and we sat while he chewed and swallowed the juice that formed in his mouth. Finally he nodded, saying there was nothing like *bell anzhelik* for soothing the throat. He said that I could have just given the root to Edmond, but I was a good granddaughter to come out into the cold night for his sake.

I thought he might tell me a story for my diary, or that perhaps he might have more to say about the battle, but he said nothing until I was almost out the door. "Isadore Dumont dead. August, Joseph Montour, Jean-Baptiste. All dead. All good men. Good friends. And Assiyiwin. He was almost blind, Josephine! He was old. Just doing what Chief Beardy sent him to do, just acting as a peacemaker. How can you reason with men who will kill a nearly blind old man, one who is not even armed?" Then he spat. "The time for peacemaking has passed."

Très tard

Before we said the rosary tonight, Papa told us that most of our men thought the battle had been an easy victory. He was not so sure. We should prepare ourselves for hard times, and we should pray for peace. It was always worth praying for.

After our prayers, Louise said that she and I must visit the households of the dead men tomorrow — they would need what strength we could give them. Then she clasped my hand, just the way she did this morning. I cannot be sure, but I do believe I may feel a slight bond growing between us. Perhaps, though, it is my imagination.

Le 27 mars 1885

Edmond and Moushoom went to visit *mo nook* Gerard. Papa would not permit me to go with them. He prefers that I stay close to home. Besides, he says,

Louise does not feel quite like herself. Weeks ago, this would have made me cross, but somehow today it did not. I can see that Papa is fond of Louise — I am not, although I will admit only here that perhaps I am beginning to like her a little — and he could be content if it were not for all the troubles. So I busied myself with working around the house. Later I spent an hour hooking Mama's rug. It soothes me, that rug.

Le 28 mars 1885

Our poor men who died at Duck Lake were buried today, and now rest at St. Laurent. The funerals were very sad, as all funerals are, but somehow these were sadder. It is one thing to be taken by disease or old age. These men, though, gave their lives for our cause. Would I be as brave if called upon to do so? I pray I never have to find out.

Le 29 mars 1885

An interesting thing. There were four priests at the Palm Sunday Mass this morning — Père Moulin, of course, but also Père Touze, Père Fourmond and Père Végréville. It is Père Végréville who founded our mission of St. Antoine four years ago.

Père Moulin gave out the *rameaux* to each of us, although of course we have no palm trees here.

However, we do have wild sage and so he passed out stalks of that. I have never seen a palm tree. I am not even certain what one looks like, but I cannot image it smells sweeter than our sage.

The priests. Some believe they are here simply as Père Moulin's guests. Papa says it is more likely that they are the "guests" of *le petit provisoire* — they were arrested yesterday so that they can be watched. It makes me feel cold inside to think that even our priests might not be trusted. Surely Monsieur Riel will be able to discover otherwise.

Once we were home, I gave my *rameaux* to Moushoom. As he always does, he broke off a bit and put it into the stove's flames, as if a thunderstorm was coming. That way we are protected. If only it could protect us from other things.

We have heard that because of the fighting at Duck Lake, the police and the people abandoned Fort Carlton yesterday and have gone to Prince Albert. That is nothing to us, but the fort caught fire by accident and burned while they were leaving. I fear we Métis will be blamed for that, even though not a one of us was there.

Le 30 mars 1885

Armand wants to go back to school. This is not because of Louise or me. It is because he misses his friends. It will be Papa's decision, but he does not have to listen to Armand whine all day.

To quiet the whining we walked down past Moushoom's cabin to the river. There is still a good deal of ice and the water is very low. It seems to me that a boat like the *Northcote* would easily run aground these days.

Le 31 mars 1885

Perhaps it would be better to throw this diary into the fire rather than write of what is happening.

Adrian rushed in after supper. He had gone over to Garnot's to hear the news and bring any back. He told us that *le petit provisoire* has declared that Monsieur Riel is a prophet. This I cannot understand. There are prophets in the Bible, but here at Batoche? Such things are beyond me, and I could see doubt in Papa's eyes as well. He kept his opinion to himself, though, and only asked Adrian if that was all he had heard. It was not. Something had been found at Duck Lake after the battle. Papers. Proof that Macdonald's army is coming. We must prepare ourselves.

Armand will not be going back to school.

Le 1 avril 1885

Edmond says that people at One Arrow's reserve are talking about Big Tom Hourie. I wondered aloud if it was because he is so tall, but that was not the reason. They say he is now carrying messages for the government's army. Some say they saw him swim across the Saskatchewan to take a message to government men in Prince Albert. Moushoom said it was idle talk and nonsense. No one could swim across and back through all that ice.

"Maybe he walked across," said Armand.

Tom Hourie *is* very tall. As serious as the matter was, I must admit that Armand's words made a very funny picture in my mind.

I cannot stop thinking about it. Not about the ice, or the walking through the river, but about people who would betray their own friends and neighbours to help Macdonald's army. Papa says that loyalty is different for everyone, and that it is difficult to understand how a person will chose one thing over another. I am not so sure. Loyalty seems a very simple thing to me. It is what I feel for my family.

Le 2 avril 1885

Holy Thursday. A wet and snowy day, suitable only for staying inside at home. This evening after we said the rosary together, I worked on Mama's rug for a while. I suddenly realize that I have not described the rug. It is a small one that measures two feet by three feet. In the centre are seven roses. I remember watching Mama draw the roses, and hearing her say that they stood for the seven of us. All around the roses are vines and leaves. "This is our home, our place," Mama explained. "Nothing can change that any more than cutting back a vine will stop the roses from returning."

Mama. How she loved Batoche.

Le 3 avril 1885

Vawndarzee Saen always seems like such a sad and lonely day to me, this day on which *Le Boon Jeu* died for our sins. After Mass we spent a quiet afternoon that suited the seriousness of the day. It was so peaceful. For a little while I could not imagine anything that could end that peacefulness.

Later Papa went over to visit Monsieur Dumont. The Dumonts are staying at Monsieur Letendre's house for the sake of convenience, as the parlour is the place from which Gabriel is commanding our army. Papa also visited the Riels, who are now living in a small house here at Batoche, one owned by Joseph Fisher.

Marguerite Riel. She has given up so much for the sake of the Métis people.

Le 4 avril 1885

Adrian brought a newspaper from Garnot's. Here is some of what it said about us.

> OTTAWA, March 23. — Immediately after routine proceedings in the House to-day, Mr. BLAKE made inquiries from the Government respecting the reported outbreak among the half-breeds at Fort Carlton.
>
> Sir JOHN MACDONALD, in reply, said that it was true that a disturbance among the half-breeds under the leadership of Louis Riel had taken place. They cut the wires and stopped communication between Qu'Appelle and the Saskatchewan. Several operators and officials had been taken prisoners. One wire had since been repaired. The immediate cause of the outbreak was not kown, but a telelgram received said it was owing to a letter sent from one of the departments which stated that Riel was not a British subject. Inquiry in the departments had failed to discover that such a letter

had been sent. It was true, however, that certain questions in connection with the half-breeds' complaints were under consideration and remain unsettled. Some of them were unreasonable and could not be entertained, but others were in process of readjustment. No bill of rights had ever been forwarded to the Government. Sir John denied

When I read it aloud in our kitchen, Papa said we should not pay any attention, and that maybe Adrian should stop bringing newspapers here. Newspapers were supposed to be the writings of educated men, but something must have gone wrong in Ottawa if that was the sort of thinking education has created. Papa added that I could make a better newspaper than this . . . this . . . and then he faltered.

"Dilet kwyee?" Moushoom suggested, and he made that sound he makes. It took away the sting of the newspaper's words and made us all laugh, for of course the story was just so much sour milk.

Le 5 avril 1885

Père Moulin and Monsieur Riel argued after Mass this morning. Again! Monsieur Riel felt that our priest should have praised the bravery of our

Métis soldiers in his sermon. Père Moulin called Monsieur Riel a heretic. It sounded like a very foul word, like something you might hear at the forge. Later, though, Louise explained that a heretic is a person who disagrees with the teachings of the church.

Still, I refused to let their disagreement spoil such a holy day for me, and although nothing was said by any of us, I am certain my family — except perhaps Adrian, who worships Monsieur Riel — felt the same way. Still, Adrian did seem happy enough. I thought about Emma, who calls this day Easter, and hoped she was happy, too.

Louise and I set the table for eight. There are only seven of us, but an extra place was added for those who had gone on before us, as it always is on special days like *Zhour di Pawk.* Lent having ended and meat again being allowed, we enjoyed *boulets* of venison and muskrat all rolled together into small balls. There was a savoury *rababoo* with *grawdpayrs,* the dumplings tasty from simmering in the stew. *Soup di pwaw,* of course, and warm fresh *galet.*

We filled our plates and Papa filled the eighth. It was a hearty, cheerful meal. When it ended, Papa took the eighth plate and put the food into the fire, whispering as he did so.

I cannot help but wonder who was in each of our thoughts as our eyes passed over that plate and the empty chair. Papa was surely thinking about Mama. Did Moushoom recall his wives or perhaps all his friends, dead these many years, some of them just recently killed at Duck Lake? And Louise. Had memories of her first husband come to mind? In any case, she did not eat much and her face was pale.

I thought of Mama, as I have each time we have set and filled that plate since she has been gone. Then sometimes I think about relatives who have passed on. This time I did not. This time I thought of the men who died at Duck Lake, men whose faces I had seen since I was a small girl. But then I could not stop myself from thinking of the others — the soldiers, and the volunteers. Were their wives and children now doing the same? I felt shame at my disloyalty. Those men might have killed Papa or Moushoom, Edmond or Adrian! I vow I will try to harden my heart. I must and I will, but somehow I think Mama would not be very happy about that.

Le 6 avril 1885

They say that Macdonald's army is only a few hundred miles away. Their leader's name is General Middleton, this soldier who means to destroy everything I hold dear.

Le 7 avril 1885

Very cold weather today. Will the cold slow down an army?

Le 8 avril 1885

How strange the way a family behaves sometimes, as though it has only one brain. We did not speak of preparations and yet today we all worked as one. Perhaps the cold rather than fear has spurred us on. Adrian melted lead and poured it into bullet moulds, working slowly so as not to waste a bit. Papa went over to Louise's old house with the sleigh — the house is not yet rented out — and when he returned he had all the pots and kettles from the kitchen. I wondered why, for a moment, and then realized that Adrian could use the lead linings to make more bullets if they were needed. I tried not to think about those bullets, or about the bullets that General Middleton's army would have. The thought of them made me feel ill.

Louise and I took stock of the cellars, and the work helped ease my mind. Most of the food was in the big cellar under the floor of this house, but a bit of flour, some potatoes and containers of seeds for the kitchen garden are stored in the small cellar beneath Moushoom's cabin. We counted the jars of preserves and checked the butter, flour and peas stored in their stone crocks. Going through each of the wooden bins of vegetables, we set aside those potatoes, carrots or turnips that were a bit shrivelled, to use soonest. Then we dusted everything and put fresh straw on the floors. Armand helped, insisting that he would hunt down and kill any rats or mice, even though they cannot get in because of the rocks that line the walls. Finally Louise sent the little hunter outside, saying that it was a clear cold day and the fresh air would do Armand good.

All the while, she and I could hear the faint sounds of hammering and sawing outside the house. When we came up, Papa called to us to see what he had made. Shutters for the windows! Now the precious panes of glass will be better protected from hail or stones. Or anything else that might hit them, although I forced *that* thought out of my head. Louise and I swept the floors, and then moved furniture away from the windows, saying how much better it all looked. Moushoom and Edmond again sharpened all the axes and knives, and then Moushoom cleaned and polished *Gárso Zhounn* until his brass gleamed like gold.

It makes me feel empty inside to write this, but we are ready.

Le 9 avril 1885

UPON THE NORTHWESTERN RANGES

They are a nomadic people, and can live in tents during the severest seasons, subsisting on jerked meat and pemmican, which is their natural food. As they follow hunting for a living they are armed with the latest pattern of repeating and breach-loading rifles, are dead shots, and could but secure an abundance of ammunition by the capture of the posts referred to. If they resist the constituted authorities by a resort to arms they will prove a very formidable foe to mounted police and undisciplined volunteers. In fact, they would make it warm for British regulars of the line.

I read this aloud to my family today.

Later, when Papa went to call Armand in for supper, instead of shouting to him Papa stood in the doorway and watched. He laughed a little and said we should come quietly and see something the newspaper story must have inspired.

There was Armand marching around the yard, a stick over his shoulder, Eagle and a few chickens following him. "I am Gabriel Dumont!" Armand shouted at the chickens. "Leave this place, you weak stupid soldiers, or I will make it warm for you." He aimed the stick at the chickens and made the sound of gunshots, which made Eagle bark and bark.

All the men laughed. Louise smiled, but it was a smile that she made only with her lips. Her eyes were serious, and when they met mine, I know she saw the same thing. Worry. But Armand was coming in, Papa was talking about the good smells, and supper must be put on the table. I sent worry away, out to where the chickens scratched in the snow.

It is the second time I have felt a bond with Louise, and this time I am certain I have not imagined it.

Le 10 avril 1885

During the night, the ice on the river disappeared. It has always seemed special to see this, as though spring is flowing in with the river's water. Today, though, all I could think of was what else might be coming up the Saskatchewan.

Le 12 avril 1885

Frogs. I heard peepers this evening. Such a sweet sound, but all sweetness disappeared when Edmond arrived with yet more terrible news. A telegram came to the office at Clarke's Crossing earlier. It said that on *le 2 avril* there had been a massacre at a place called Frog Lake, perhaps two hundred miles to the west. Nine white settlers were killed, including two priests and the Indian agent. Edmond said he was told that it was some of Big Bear's young Cree warriors who were responsible for the killings.

Moushoom told us that he had not talked to Big Bear in years. He went on to say that Big Bear is a good chief, a man who always tried to do the right thing by his people. He talked about how the Cree were truly starving out there, and how starvation does strange things to a man, when he sees his wife and children waste away. So much suffering and so much hunger among all the tribes since the buffalo have stopped coming.

Papa wondered what Monsieur Riel must think, and although I wondered the same thing, none of us could guess. Now, I am certain that somehow we will be blamed for this. Two hundred miles, a thousand miles. No matter.

The thought of it is so frightening.

Le 13 avril 1885

Waiting. Only waiting.

Le 15 avril 1885

When Adrian came in this afternoon, his lip was swollen and bloody. Someone had struck him a blow to the mouth. Papa was angry, very angry, as he disapproves of fistfights, but he did not press Adrian. Finally, after a quiet and melancholy supper, the words poured out of Adrian, the way pus will pour from a boil when it is lanced.

The split lip? He was in a fight outside of Garnot's. Papa asked him who he had fought. Then Adrian straightened up and his eyes flashed. A *Kanayah,* he told us, a freighter from Prince Albert who had the manners of a pig. "I taught him new manners," Adrian said.

Once Armand was asleep, Adrian told us more. He said it had been a matter of name calling. Once I heard what my brother had been called, I understood. *Batochien.* Moushoom observed that it was a bad word, a slur against what we are, but it was only a word after all. Words can only take on the power you let them take on.

Adrian probably did not heed any of *those* words. He hides it, but I am certain that he is still so sad about Emma.

Plus tard

There was friendship growing between Emma and I. We might have become closer, but I think that more than a river divides us now. Only here will I admit that I am sad too.

Le 17 avril 1885

More snow fell today, but the weather also brought something else. Finally, something good has come out of the troubles, and what excitement it has caused. Nuns! Four women of the Faithful Companions of Jesus, the nuns who taught at St. Laurent, have come to stay here. It seems they were on their way to Calgary, since the bishop feared for their safety. That part of the news I did not like, but I suppose the bishop must think the nuns are in more danger than ordinary people are these days. No matter. Back to the news.

Somehow Monsieur Riel got word to the nuns that they had nothing to fear, that they would be completely safe in Batoche. Papa says that Monsieur Riel's mama wanted to be a nun before she married, and of course his sister Sara was a nun herself. Monsieur Riel has a tender spot in his heart for nuns, I think.

One part of the news I greatly enjoyed. While on the road, one of the wheels of their wagon broke. Now, I did not like to hear that, but the part that comes after, because it was not the driver who repaired the wheel. It was one of the *nuns,* Mother Mary Greene, who came here from Ireland years ago.

The nuns were taken to Monsieur Letendre's house, since it is the finest home here, and Madame Dumont and Madame Letendre saw to the nuns' comfort. They will be staying at the rectory though, since it is near the church.

When Armand heard that Mother Mary Greene came from Ireland, he added her to the picture that Louise drew for him. He says that when he meets this Mother Greene he will ask her if she knows the Fenian slaves.

I had to turn away my face when I heard that. Armand's picture is becoming very messy and it looks foolish, but anything he does that keeps him from being afraid is good.

Monsieur Riel says the nuns will be safe. I pray that it means we too will be safe.

Le 18 avril 1885

The camps around Batoche are now full of people who think that they will be protected from General Middleton's soldiers if they are here. I pity them, for they all look so frightened and lost. These men, women and children have placed their faith in Monsieur Riel. It must be a heavy burden for him to bear.

Le 19 avril 1885

I find myself searching the horizon, what I can see of it. My ears almost hurt from listening for anything unusual. What does an army sound like?

Le 20 avril 1885

Papa has heard that the MacLeods' house is empty. It was hard to watch Adrian's face when Papa gave us that news.

Le 21 avril 1885

I keep thinking about Emma and that empty house. It seems to me that nothing is as lonely as an empty house with its dark windows. I am not certain what will happen here, but our house is filled, and not only with people.

Le 22 avril 1885

We are all sleeping downstairs. Moushoom did not want to leave his cabin, so Papa had to be very firm about how we must stay as close together as we can. To my great relief, Moushoom saw the sense in that. Edmond is living here in the big house as well, naturally. For the sake of modesty, Louise and I will share the bedroom, and all the men will sleep in the kitchen. Modesty does not seem so very important at the moment, somehow, not with an army coming our way.

Le 23 avril 1885

All our men except for Moushoom left tonight for Tourond's Coulee downriver past Gabriel's Crossing, a place the English call Fish Creek. Someone must stay back with Armand and the women, Papa insisted. This made Armand cross. Nothing would please him more than joining in the fight, he says.

Moushoom was not very pleased either. His blood was up, but when Papa said that Moushoom was the best shot and the most fearless, he calmed himself and agreed to remain here. This time.

It was very hard to watch them ride away, but I put on a brave face and the best smile I could manage. Even when Papa embraced Louise, although now that I think about it, something about that embrace touched me somehow.

None of us except Armand can sleep.

Le 24 avril 1885

Some of the men feared for their families, so Monsieur Riel led them back here in the early hours of morning. Papa, Edmond and Adrian were not among them. Not knowing that they are safe is almost impossible to bear. I am too unsettled to write more. Mama's rug. Just holding it will help.

Plus tard

We can hear the fighting. A heavy wet snow is falling, but it cannot blanket the sounds of gunshots and cannon. Louise put her arm around my shoulder as we stood at the window. Weeks ago I would have pulled away, but today I did not, for I know she loves Papa and the others as much as I do.

What does an army sound like? It sounds like a monster.

Encore plus tard

Papa and our men are safely home, thank *Le Boon Jeu*.

People are saying that it was a victory for us down at Tourond's Coulee where the battle took place. That it was something to see what a hundred and fifty or so Métis had done to seven or eight hundred soldiers. Papa is not so sure. We fought well, he agreed, and yes, Middleton's soldiers withdrew, but so did we. Papa says our losses were great — four brave Métis dead, some wounded, and fifty-five horses killed. Moushoom does not think the men will be able to fight on the way they need to, for what is a Métis without a horse? I could hear the disbelief in his voice as he repeated the terrible number. Fifty-five. Fifty-five gone.

They say Monsieur Riel and many of the village women prayed together all the way through the battle. He held his arms out so that he formed a cross. When he tired, the women took turns supporting his arms. I am sure Louise prayed to herself while we waited here. I know I did. Now I will pray for the souls of those killed tonight. And I will give thanks that our family is whole.

Le 25 avril 1885

They are digging trenches and what Papa calls rifle pits on the prairie between Batoche and the church. Our men used trenches at Tourond's Coulee and so they will surely work here.

Moushoom took Louise, Armand and me over in the wagon to watch the men digging. The pits are shallow, less than two feet deep, but they are each protected by a log embankment. Our men will be able to see the enemy coming long before the soldiers suspect who is hiding in wait for them.

When we returned home, Louise took to her bed. She said the movement of the wagon had upset her stomach a little. She insisted that it was nothing, but it seemed like something to me. Perhaps some tea will help settle her stomach. I will stop writing and see to it.

Le 26 avril 1885

People are beginning to abandon their houses. Some women are digging hiding places in or near the riverbank. Others are preparing to camp in a sheltered area surrounded by bluffs. The nights are so cold. I fear they will freeze.

We will remain here. None of us will consider abandoning our home.

Au point du jour

I have had a dream, a horrible dream. Most of it is gone now, thank *Le Boon Jeu,* but enough of it remains. Even when I squeeze my eyes closed, I can still see the men digging the long deep pits. It was no one from here who was digging, though. It was men in red coats, men with silver eyes. One of them looked at me, and even though he did not speak, I could hear his words in my head. *Do not worry, Josephine,* he said. *I am digging a fine deep one for you.*

That was when I woke. I know now that the soldier was not digging a hiding place for me. He was digging a grave.

Le 27 avril 1885

Our men take turns searching the countryside for Middleton's army. Only when the scouting parties return and Papa or Moushoom or Edmond or Adrian walk into the kitchen does my heart slow.

Le 29 avril 1885

Indian women and children are now coming in to Batoche too, although there are few warriors. Only White Cap and perhaps twenty of his men are camped just north of Batoche.

We, like our neighbours, have had to give many of our cattle to help feed all of these people. Papa did this willingly but I know he is worried. It is not just the cattle. We have made no preparations at all to plant this year's crops. Monsieur Dumont has decreed that no man will till the soil. The temptation to farm rather than fight might be too great.

By now the kitchen garden should have been planned, the seeds readied. Knowing this, Louise and I pulled away the mulch and spent the afternoon picking through the seeds. She could barely do the work, though. Her face became slick with sweat, she said her stomach felt sick, and so went back into the house. It worries me to see her feeling so unwell.

Le 30 avril 1885

The thought of no food is frightening, but so is the fact that there is little ammunition for the guns of our soldiers, though we hear that many of the women have been melting down their pots and making as many bullets as they can. Moushoom has a fine rifle. Adrian and Papa are well armed, but some of our men have only old-fashioned muskets or duck guns. They are good enough for hunting, but if you are ~~hunting men~~

I must not think of people in that way. Our soldiers will defend us honourably in the eyes of *Le Boon Jeu.*

Middleton's army has modern guns. Edmond has described them to me. They have cannon and something called a Gatling gun. Some of the men are saying that the Gatling gun is just so much *rababoo*, perhaps because of the noise they have heard that it makes. Edmond says that the Gatling gun does not fire. Instead, it spits out bullets, hundreds and hundreds in less than a minute. Compared to those soldiers, we may as well be armed with brooms.

No one said anything. The picture Edmond had put into our heads was too much. Armand stood, went to the corner, and picked up the kitchen broom, shouting that he was ready!

Poor little Armand.

Le 1 mai 1885

Mama's watch has stopped, an unimportant thing, I know. Papa says we must take it to a watchmaker in Prince Albert that Louise once mentioned. Northgraves is the name of the shop.

It is a small thing, but no longer being able to hear the watch's ticking is almost as though its heart has stopped.

Le 2 mai 1885

The river rose very quickly last night. Branches and logs floated past at a great speed. May this evil time pass the same way.

Le 3 mai 1885

Louise and Papa have argued. When Armand and his friends argue, there is a great deal of screaming and sometimes pinches and slaps, but that was not the case with Papa and Louise. There were no raised voices, yet I could still tell they were in disagreement.

It did not make for a very comfortable evening. Even Moushoom could feel the difference. Finally, he said he was going for a walk — if it was summer, he would almost swear a storm was coming, and perhaps he should get out the *rameaux* and throw some into the stove.

Plus tard

More arguing, and this time it truly was like a storm. Papa wants to take us — Armand, Louise and me — to Louise's sister in Prince Albert, and not for the sake of the watch, either. He wants to leave us there until the trouble has passed. I know he is only trying to protect us, but it is more important for the family to remain together. I will not go. If I have to hide in the woods and eat leaves, I will not go!

Encore plus tard

Papa and I have just spoken. I apologized for my disobedience and shouting. Then I reminded him of what people had said just before the fighting at Duck Lake, that if they had to die for their country they would all die together. When I told Papa that I understood those words now, and that I felt the same way, tears came to his eyes and to mine. His words made me cry even harder.

"My good brave Josephine," he said. "You are so much like your mother."

Tears. They hurt so much and yet when they are gone, you feel healed somehow.

Le 4 mai 1885

Only Moushoom remained behind today, for it was not his turn to go on patrol. The weather has turned warmer, but still he sat in the kitchen near the stove, *Gárso Zhounn* within reach as he wove his sash. Louise worked slowly on her knitting, and I held Mama's rug, although I had no heart to do any hooking. Armand for once was still, contenting himself with stroking Moon's head. It was all peaceful enough until Louise stood suddenly and went to the bedroom. She shut the door, but still I could hear the sound of her vomiting into a washbasin. The troubles have upset her that much, I thought. When Armand said that maybe Louise had eaten too many *bengs,* Moushoom smiled and told Armand to go down to the cabin and get his pipe.

His third wife, my grandmother, was like that, Moushoom told me when Armand was gone. I had never heard any stories about my grandmother eating too many *bengs* and then vomiting, but I suppose it is possible. Anything is. But then Moushoom said this — and I have written it exactly as he said it: "When she carried your papa in her belly, her stomach was sick almost the whole time. And she craved the livers of freshwater cod. Oh how she craved them! Then one morning he was born right there on the prairie when we were all out on the buffalo hunt. It was a relief to see that new baby, I will tell you. I was worried that when your papa finally emerged, he would have fins and gills! The women who helped your grandmother with the birth found that very amusing, as I recall."

Then he added that I should close my mouth, since with it hanging open I looked too much like a cod.

I felt so many things at that moment. Embarrassment, excitement and understanding all battled with each other. What a silly girl I was not to have read the signs. Not that I knew them so well, but Nohkom LaBute *had* poured tea in this house not long after the wedding. Everyone knows that when a woman pours tea in another woman's home, the wife of the house will soon become pregnant. Just then, Armand rushed in with Moushoom's pipe and Louise came out of the bedroom, her face as pale as milk.

I have thought about this all day and evening. I could not help but watch Papa when he and the others came home, but Papa looked the same. It is not he who will change, I suppose. It must be the reason he wants us to go to Prince

Plus tard

Louise knocked on my door a few minutes ago. She had something to tell me, she said. Not the baby. She knew that I was old enough to understand such things, after all. Babies were just part of life. It was the other matter, the matter of Prince Albert.

She will not go. This child will be born here in Batoche, in our house, and not even General Middleton can change that. He had best think twice before crossing Louise Pepin Bouvier's path. And Josephine's, she added.

I embraced her then, not as my mother, but as

the mother of my unborn brother or sister, and as a friend.

Le 5 mai 1885

Papa brought this from Monsieur Letendre's store today. It was in a Winnipeg newspaper.

—AND—

We Are Laughing

Because we can Sell You

GOODS

FROM THE

Largest AND Best Stock!

IN THE CITY FOR

LESS MONEY

Than Any Other House.

JUST RECEIVED

RIEL

GIVING THE LAUGH

—TO—

MIDDLETON'S

BIG FORCE!

—AND—

We Are Laughing

Because we can Sell You

GOODS

FROM THE

Largest AND Best Stock!

IN THE CITY FOR

LESS MONEY

Than Any Other House

JUST RECEIVED

LATEST STYLES IN STETSON'S HATS

CALL AND SEE THEM

BROWN & COBLENTZ,

Champion Clothiers & Merchant Tailors

COR. MAIN AND LOGAN STS.

I suppose that people in Winnipeg are cheering us on. I do not see what there is to laugh about, though.

There has been no more talk of leaving.

Le 6 mai 1885

It is likely that every woman in Batoche knows about Louise's pregnancy, especially since Nohkom LaBute came to visit today. Mama used to say that Nohkom made her think of a dandelion that scatters its seeds everywhere as soon as even a puff of wind touches it. That is how Nohkom scatters news.

She also brought news, though. Madame Riel sent her congratulations, one pregnant woman to another. Yes, Nohkom told us, Marguerite Riel is with child. And with her congratulations, she had sent a gift for Louise's baby, a tiny pair of wristlets that she had crocheted from blue and white yarn.

Marguerite Riel must be a very kind woman to think of Louise at a time such as this, with war threatening. Moushoom says that women fight a different sort of war when they are with child. Their spirits do battle for the little one inside of them.

I must try to be more helpful to Louise.

Le 7 mai 1885

Middleton's army is very close. Word has reached us that his men are breaking into farmhouses and looting them, and what they cannot carry away, they destroy. Not even the white settlers are safe from those soldiers. It takes all my will to keep the worry I am feeling hidden inside me.

They burned Gabriel Dumont's house and tore down his stable. Nothing remains. They took his billiard table, Madame Dumont's washing machine, and even some of her clothing onto the *Northcote!* What will an army do with a washing machine and woman's clothing? For shame! As for the *Northcote,* it is now an army steamer and Monsieur Dumont has told Papa that it will surely be used against us. Papa says the army will be here soon, and that we are to take heart and place our trust in *Le Boon Jeu*. He says the *Northcote* is in for a big surprise.

Tard le soir

I can almost smell the fear that hangs over Batoche.

Le 8 mai 1885

A difficult day. Papa and the others are gone, for they are part of our army. Monsieur Dumont has planned Batoche's defence, and all the men are needed to carry it out. Moushoom said that we must keep the dogs close, that Moon will defend us.

The waiting is terrible. I want the fighting to begin so that it will be over with, yet I do not want it to begin at all. No wanting will keep Middleton away, though. No prayers will slow him and his soldiers. Oh, to be a man so that I too could fight!

Le 9 mai 1885

At around eight o'clock this morning, the *Northcote* passed by our farm. In happier times, Armand and I would stand on the riverbank, Armand gesturing and shouting to the captain so that he would blow the whistle. Not today. Today we watched in silence from an upstairs window as the steamer and two barges passed by. When the steamer was almost at the church, our men fired from both sides of the river. The *Northcote* slowed — perhaps it had hit one of the sandbars — and then it happened. The surprise! Our men drew up a stout cable that they had stretched across the river and down came the steamer's smokestacks. Away it floated.

We heard the sound of a soldier's bugle, and the battle began in earnest. That was when we hurried downstairs to where Papa had told us to go. We sat on the floor at the back wall of the house, hoping the stove would give us protection. The dogs huddled near us, trembling and panting — all except Moon, who just stared ahead calmly. Now and again, there would be a whiz or a thump as bullets hit or nicked the house, and then poor little Eagle would whine.

Louise sat with a hand over her belly. Armand put his fingers in his ears and squeezed his eyes shut.

Nothing will happen to us, I told myself again and

again. I should scratch that out, for the truth is that I have never been so afraid in all my life, never so certain I would be killed, and yet the fear I felt for Papa and the others was greater.

Later, when it was dark and the battle had stopped, Adrian crept home to give us news and assure us that Papa, Moushoom and Edmond were unharmed. To my shame, I burst into tears upon hearing this, and I know my shame must have showed. My face was so hot.

Adrian paid no attention, only saying that Gabriel had hoped for more but it was still a victory, for the *Northcote* had fled with its tail between its legs. He insisted that the battle had been fun! What if the soldiers did fire their cannons? Not one Métis was killed. In fact, Adrian and the others had amused themselves by making dummies and using them to draw the enemy's fire. It had worked, for the dummies were now filled with bullets. And the bravery of our men! Some of them tried to capture one of the Gatling guns. That they failed was meaningless, for it was the trying that counted.

Père Moulin had been shot in the leg, although it was not a serious wound. The priests had run up a white flag on the church, Adrian said. They had surrendered — the cowards — and for all he knew were giving information to Middleton. Adrian said he would tell Papa we were fine. Then he snatched up a piece of *galet* and was gone, asking us to pray for them all.

Surely the priests and nuns will not abandon us!

Plus tard

Louise says that my tears are nothing to be ashamed of. All they mean is that I have a tender heart, and that I love my family greatly.

Louise. I think that perhaps she also deserves some of that love.

Le 10 mai 1885

More fighting. I am so afraid for our men.

Plus tard

Edmond came to us tonight with a message from Papa. They are very short of ammunition and so we are to melt down everything that can be used to make bullets for them. There must be something left. This we did with Edmond's help, melting down the foil from old tea chests, some tin plates and even our teakettles.

Edmond said that Monsieur Dumont is having our men pick up bullets and cartridge belts that the enemy have dropped. And, of course, they take the guns of the dead. I wish he had not told us that.

If anything

Juin

Le 25 juin 1885

I never thought to see Edmond Swift Fox again, much less this diary, after more than a month. But there he was this morning, although now he has left us once more. And the news he brought! I cannot stand

Plus tard

Write it all, Moushoom told me when I began this diary. It seems so long ago that he said those words. The very thought of all the things that have happened, and the fact of Edmond's return, so moved my heart that writing was beyond me. Now I have settled myself, and I think I may be able to do what my grandfather once instructed. *Write it all.*

To do so I must return to last month, and I would rather never have seen this diary again than do that. But I am an obedient granddaughter.

So. That night in *mai,* Moushoom ran into the house and interrupted my writing. Edmond was with him. Moushoom told us that Monsieur Riel planned to send a letter to Middleton, insisting that if any women or children were killed, he would massacre the white prisoners that the Métis were holding.

Moushoom said that Papa did not trust Middleton, though, and neither did he, so we must go down to the river immediately and hide in Armand's cave, his Fort Bouvier behind the cabin. There was to be no argument. We were to leave everything behind.

I remember how I felt just then. Afraid, of course, but with that fear was anger. This was my *home.* How could I just hand it over to Middleton?

Moushoom meant his words, though. He did not even give me time to take my diary as he and Edmond pulled us out of the house, past his cabin and into Armand's fort.

"Stay here," Moushoom ordered. "Do not come out no matter what you hear."

I could hardly bear it when Moushoom left, saying he would not let his son and grandson fight alone, that the Bouviers would stand together. "Keep your will strong, Josephine," he whispered. I told him that I would. But then Edmond said that if he were to die, he would die at the side of those he loved, and my will failed me. I wept, saying

Plus tard

I have wept again at those memories.

So. Back to that day in *mai* again. At first, it was dark. Then the sun rose, and so did the sounds of the fighting.

It was the same the next day as the Gatling gun

clattered, the cannon roared and the cries of wounded and dying men haunted us. Two days passed. I crept to Moushoom's cabin by darkness. There was water in a jug and those few vegetables in the cellar, but we used them sparingly. Even Armand did not complain. Louise and I held him between us, and I know we gave him strength. We prayed together, and so hard did I entreat God and all the saints that most of the sounds had stopped before I even noticed.

It was then that we heard Moushoom outside, cursing.

We climbed from the cave, peeked through the trees, and saw

Encore plus tard

So hard to write this.

The soldiers had taken what they wanted, and then set fire to our house and Louise's house, the stable and barn. Even from where we hid in the trees I could see them carrying off our belongings and food. One soldier had a cooking pot on his head, and was wearing Papa's finest coat, the one Mama had embroidered. Chairs, the table, our dishes — all lay broken in the yard. Our mattresses and pillows had been cut open and the feathers scattered everywhere.

I might have stood all this, even though my anger was so great. We ran to Moushoom and as we did so, he fell to his knees, weeping over the bodies of his dogs. Bone, Willow and even little Eagle were dead, shot by the soldiers. Moushoom was sure they had died fighting. Of Moon, there was no sign. And where were Papa, Edmond and Adrian? we all asked at once.

Edmond is missing, wept my grandfather. Papa and Adrian had been arrested. He himself had been arrested too, but then released, although the soldiers had kept his rifle. The men of the Council had also been arrested and taken away, he told us.

"But the *councillors* were the leaders," I said, "powerful men. Papa and Adrian were not part of the Council." But Moushoom said they would still be tried, just as the Council would be tried.

None of it made sense.

If they were lucky, Moushoom said, Papa and Adrian would be released.

And if they were unlucky? We all wanted to ask it, but none of us did.

By evening, the fires were dead. Nothing could be saved. La Mignonne, the chickens, the goats, the cats, the horses — all dead or run off, mad with fear. Papa's fiddle, Mama's rug, her sash and watch, Louise's books, the diaries, the ledger — all turned to ashes. What food the soldiers had left in the cellar had been destroyed when the burning floor caved in.

Moushoom buried the dogs, refusing anyone's

help, and then we walked back to his cabin. I remember only misery rather than gratitude that it was well hidden by the trees. The soldiers would have burned it and the shed too, had they noticed such small buildings. What could you expect of men who were low enough to have stolen the very bell from our church? Yes! I will write it again. They stole Marie-Antoinette and carried her away from Batoche.

We spent the first of many nights there in the cabin, but of all those nights, it was the saddest. We had nothing now, and that was bad enough, but we feared for Papa and Adrian. And no one knew whether Edmond was alive. Moushoom had searched among the wounded and even looked at the dead, but Edmond was not among them.

Enough. I can write no more tonight.

Le 26 juin 1885

I will finish this.

In the days that followed, we learned that Monsieur Riel had surrendered. Hearing the news, Gabriel Dumont fled to the United States, leaving Madame Dumont with his father. I remember Armand saying that maybe Edmond and Moon were with Monsieur Dumont, but I did not think so. In my heart I was sure they both lay dead somewhere.

Some were saying that Big Tom Hourie and two other men claimed to have captured Louis Riel, but that was not correct. After the battle, Monsieur Riel had hidden for three days in the cellar of a farmhouse maybe thirty miles from here. On the third day he surrendered by his own choice, and no capturing was involved. Moushoom's words of so many months ago had come true. This time Louis Riel had not run in the end.

Some said that in an act of gratitude he gave his sash to the people who had hidden him. Even now, I do not know if that was correct, but Moushoom said it sounded like something Louis would do. What was true was that now Monsieur Riel was on his way to Regina for trial.

The army's Gatling gun had taken the life of

Plus tard

It hurts so much to write these bitter words, but write them I will. Once I thought that no one would ever read this diary. Now I hope the whole country reads it, that Macdonald reads it and knows what he did to us.

The soldiers killed Marcile Gratton, an innocent girl of ten years who had only been trying to reach her mother. Thirteen of our men were killed, Joseph Ouellette among them. Ninety-three years old and he had still been a match for any of Middleton's soldiers, right to the end! As for the dead redcoats, the army had taken the bodies of those soldiers with them, all except one man who had no family back east to claim him. That soldier they had buried not far from Monsieur Caron's house near the river. When I heard that, I felt ill at the thought that even one soldier would remain here in our land.

The church and some of the merchants' buildings were spared by the soldiers, because those men had not fought against the army. There was no mercy for those who had, however, and so Middleton's men burned almost every Métis farmhouse. The stink of it comes back to me again as I write this.

There was little or no food, of course, for no crops had been planted. We had more supplies than many — some flour and a bag of potatoes, a few cabbages that had been stored in Moushoom's small cellar — but that would not last all summer. There were the seeds, corn, beans and peas, and so we would try to make do with that, but both Louise and I worried whether it would be enough. We decided we would plant a garden, no matter how hard that would be without a plough or a horse. Moushoom would fish and hunt. We would cut wood and add onto the cabin, build another barn, start again. Somehow we would do it. It was mostly brave talk, I know now, but the words gave us the strength to do the little we could.

Mai turned to *juin,* and although the tiny garden was growing, it would be a long while before anything could be harvested. We looked to the land in other ways. If so many people had not left Batoche, it would have been impossible to find anything at all, but they had gone and so our chances were better. Louise and I dug cattail and burdock roots. When boiled they could be eaten. Armand hunted for crayfish in the river's shallows while Moushoom tried to spear fish. We were always hungry, but unlike others, we were not forced to do terrible things. Some, like the Letendres, were eating their dogs. I could almost give thanks that Moushoom's dogs were dead.

It was hard, but for Louise and the child she carried, it was harder. Nothing seemed to fill her. She needed meat, but there was none, and the helplessness I felt then tore at me day and night.

One evening while we were eating a poor supper of fish broth, we heard a small sound outside. Armand said he was sure it was the ghost of that dead soldier buried near the river, but Moushoom said he doubted it. The soldiers had done enough damage to Batoche in life. It was unlikely any of them would bother us in death. Perhaps it was an animal — a raccoon, or a squirrel — and if it was, if Moushoom could kill it, we would have meat. He slowly crept to the door, an axe in his hand, ready for whatever creature was there. "Open it," he whispered to me. I did. And there was Moon.

All of us wept. Moon was thin and one of his paws was cut and had become infected, but he was still the dog we had known. He did not whimper or snap while Moushoom cleaned and bandaged his paw. This finished, Moushoom gave him the last of his soup. Moon ate it, curled up and went to sleep near the stove. It was so good to have that dog back. I think that some of the bitterness in me drained away at that moment.

Late that night I woke. Moushoom sat near Moon, stroking his head. "Thank you, my old friend," he said again and again. "Thank you for offering yourself to us in our time of need."

I said not a word to anyone, not in the morning, not during the day, but although Armand suspected nothing, Louise somehow knew. If Moushoom could do what he must, if he could be that brave, so would I. Surely I could be that brave.

But when he said that he thought he would take a walk with his dog, when he clucked his tongue and Moon went to him so willingly, it was too much. "There is no need," I said to him, but Moushoom only smiled and told me that there was a need.

I will never forget the sadness in his voice. I knew that I should think of Louise's unborn *bābee,* and of my father. He would want to see his new child in time, and Adrian would want to see his brother or sister. He knew that Moon was ready, and for that we should be thankful. I could not watch Moushoom pick up his axe and leave the cabin, Moon limping at his heel.

I think I have never felt such despair. When Armand asked what Moushoom was doing, and Louise told him, he sobbed and sobbed. I wanted to follow Moushoom, to drive Moon away, or to take the axe. I had to do *something,* but instead I did nothing. I would like to write that I am an obedient granddaughter, but at that moment I believe I was just a coward.

We heard a long howl and then nothing. *It is done, coward,* I told myself.

But then there were voices, shouts, and Moon was barking and Moushoom was crying that Edmond had returned! Edmond was here!

Edmond had a small antelope slung across his saddle, a young doe that he had come upon not an hour ago. How I thanked that animal as Edmond and Moushoom skinned it, as Louise and I cut it into pieces and later as we filled our bellies. There was meat and there would be soup and stew for days.

And there was news.

Edmond had followed Papa, Adrian and the other prisoners to Prince Albert, staying well hidden so that he would not be taken himself. In time, all the prisoners were sent to Regina and yet again

Edmond had followed. He had not seen Papa or Adrian except from a distance, but he was certain they were well enough. The jail in Regina was a terrible place, but they did not suffer alone. Monsieur Riel's trial was to begin soon, Edmond had heard, probably next month.

Then Edmond, overtaken by his emotion, cried that Middleton and the government must be blind as well as stupid. Louise agreed, wondering how Riel could be tried for fighting when he had never raised a hand unless there was a crucifix in it. I knew the answer to that. Treason. They would try him for treason. As it had so long ago, the word made me shiver.

Encore plus tard

All there is left to write about is how this diary and Mama's diary again came to be in my hands.

It was Edmond, dear good Edmond. He had returned to our house just before he and Moushoom went back to the fighting. He knew the soldiers would come and he had to save something.

Edmond handed the diaries to me, gave me these gifts, and then he took something away. How it hurt. He was riding to Regina, he told us, to wait for news of Papa and Adrian. He and I did not say goodbye, but I could not even say that I would see him again, that he must return soon. Nor could I bring myself to watch him ride away, and so the last I had of Edmond Swift Fox was the sound of his horse's hoofbeats.

Edmond. He is my good friend.

Juillet

Le 16 juillet 1885

We have heard that Big Bear surrendered to the police at Fort Carlton. Not a word from Edmond, though. I have little heart to write.

Papa and Adrian. I am so worried about them.

Août

Le 7 août 1885

One Arrow has been arrested. So has White Cap.

Pendant la nuit

Moushoom spoke to us about the battle for the first time. I know it is because of what happened to One Arrow. He and Moushoom were close, those two, from all their hunts together over the years, back when the buffalo were here.

I would rather forget my grandfather's words, but I cannot and so here they are, as well as I can recall them:

The Battle of Batoche
Told by Moushoom Thompson Bouvier

We lay in the rifle pits the men had dug. From there we could see our white flag with the image of the Holy Virgin on it as it fluttered over a store by the river. That flag cheered on the men. But Louis Riel! No rifle pit for him. He strode up and down, calling out encouragement to us as though the enemy's bullets were not flying around him. I think that the Holy Virgin herself was shielding that man and us. Even though Middleton's men shot their cannon and made a horrible noise with their Gatling gun, not a single Métis fighter had been wounded for two days. Soldiers were wounded and dead, though, and it filled my heart with joy.

The joy faded when we learned that these soldiers, these men who would have killed us, were being nursed by Père Moulin and the nuns. They even fed them! And they call Louis Riel a traitor? This same priest who swore he would not give the comfort of the sacraments to our brave men or their families was now helping the *enemy,* as were the other priests. I cannot express my disgust or that of Edmond, your father and your brother. But there was a war to fight and so we all set it aside.

As for One Arrow, he should not have been arrested. He is a chief, though, and has always behaved like one. Is that a crime?

I never thought we would win. Middleton had too many soldiers. They were better armed, and had more ammunition. Our ammunition ran out, as you know, even though you, Louise, and the other women made more. The nails and stones we had to use in our rifles at the end were not enough. When the soldiers advanced, there was nothing to do but leave the trenches. That is when our men were killed. I will not talk more about it, but I will say that they went bravely in spite of the terrible manner in which some of them died.

I know the ways of men like Macdonald. The army will march home and he will give them medals for their bravery. But it is your papa and Adrian and all the other Métis who are the true heroes. Be proud of them. We should always be proud of what they did. That is all I will ever have to say about this war.

He paused for a moment and then looked right at us. "Forgive me, Josephine and Louise," he said, "for being happy that Middleton's soldiers died, but that is what battle does to a man."

Moushoom. My dear dear grandfather. He is a hero, too.

Le 8 août 1885

Someone brought a newspaper to Monsieur Letendre's today. It did not take long for what it said to reach us here, even though there are fewer of us these days to pass along the news, Nohkom LaBute having died last week. Some say it was from a broken heart.

So. The news is that Monsieur Riel's trial is over. The jury asked for mercy, but Monsieur Riel has been sentenced to hang.

Moushoom shook his fist at the sky when he heard that. "An innocent man!" he cried. "They have sentenced an innocent man to die."

Louise said that when we prayed the rosary tonight we would pray for Monsieur Riel's soul.

I know nothing of the men who decided this. I know nothing of a world in which such things can happen, I thank *Le Boon Jeu.* But I do know that what they have done to Louis Riel is wrong. If they can do this to him, what will they do to Papa and Adrian?

Le 19 août 1885

Edmond returned tonight. He did not hold back his news, even though he must have known how it would be taken. Some days ago, One Arrow was sentenced to serve three years in a prison called

Stony Mountain, back in Manitoba. He would not be alone. They would be trying a chief called Poundmaker in time, and even though Poundmaker was innocent, he would surely be sent to the prison. That was how the law worked.

I could tell there was more. We all could. It came from Edmond reluctantly, but it did come. The other Métis had been tried. A few had been released, but the rest were found guilty and sentenced, some for seven years, some for three years, some for one. Papa and Adrian would be in the prison by now, having been taken there by train. Edmond had thought it best to wait to tell us.

In my head I could see Papa and Adrian, their faces white, their eyes searching in vain for our faces among the people watching the train pass by. In my heart I could feel their sorrow and disappointment. To my shame, I screamed at Edmond. I will not write what I said, but I will write that it drove him from the house. Later, I found him at the river, and when I begged for his forgiveness, he waved away my begging. "What is a little screaming between friends," he said.

Le 25 août 1885

Edmond is gone, but not in anger, for we spoke last night, and all is well between us. He will ride to

Winnipeg so that he can be close to Papa and Adrian until they are released. Moushoom has given him the money he will need to buy horses for them.

I have vowed many things since I began this diary. Some promises I have kept and some, I am ashamed to say, I have broken. I vow this, though. I will not write another word until Papa, Adrian and Edmond return.

Novembre

Le 17 novembre 1885

They have come home to us at last, Papa and Adrian having been let out of the prison early. Nothing I ever write can tell of our happiness and relief. Moushoom brought his bottle of brandy from the cellar and poured a little into cups for all of us. "To Louis Riel," said Papa. "He was a good man." And that is how we learned that Monsieur Riel was dead.

"They hanged him yesterday," Papa told us. He and the others had heard it on the street as they rode through Batoche. It was said he died bravely, calmly, standing straight.

"A man could do worse than to die bravely," said Moushoom, raising his glass. "To Louis Riel. May he rest in peace."

Le 19 novembre 1885

Papa brought home a letter today, two letters really, since two pieces of paper were in the envelope. One had Adrian's name on it, and on the other was written my name. I have no idea what Adrian's letter said, but I saw that he was smiling regretfully as he read it in the kitchen.

As for my letter, I will paste it here in my diary.

Dear Josephine,

I have followed what has happened over the last months. Papa brings home the newspaper every day. He is again working for the Toronto Globe, *and so I have been able to read the stories about Batoche and Louis Riel. Papa and I talk about them when Mama is not within hearing. She does not care to listen to such unpleasantness, she tells us.*

My father says that we should not judge. A jury has judged Louis Riel, and a Higher Court will judge him when he is gone. The Higher Court is God, but you know that.

Your letter said that you were faced with hard times, and that you did not know what would come of them. I suppose that is true of all of us in some ways. Still, I hope that you and your family have not suffered. No matter what happened, I remain your friend,

Emma MacLeod

Le 20 novembre 1885

Our baby was born just after dawn this morning, in the room that my grandfather added on to the cabin some months ago. He is a small baby who has Papa's green eyes and he is very noisy. Moushoom says that noisiness seems to run in this family, and that maybe he will have to move into Armand's fort. It might be crowded in the fort, though. Moushoom had put a bit of sugar out there yesterday and by nightfall, it was gone. He suspects that the *Ma-ma-kwa-se-sak* have finally returned. If he must move out, hopefully they will be somewhat quieter than certain boys and babies.

It was all in fun, for Moushoom is as happy and proud as any of us.

I could not help but think of poor Madame Riel's baby. Her little boy lived only a few hours after his birth last month in St. Boniface. Monsieur Riel went to his death without ever seeing his newborn son.

We are so blessed. In time my baby brother will be baptized Alexandre for Louise's father, and Thompson for Moushoom. Alexandre Thompson Louis Bouvier. I need not write the reason for the third name.

Tell the truth, Moushoom said to me, but I no longer seem to be able to recognize it. Once I thought that Batoche was the most quiet place in the world, and that nothing could change the way of life that had always gone on here. I was wrong. I thought that friendship could never survive what turned out to be a terrible war. I believe that at least some of it has.

As for Monsieur Riel, I do not know what to write about him any more. I read Emma's letter aloud to my family. Louise and Papa agreed that Monsieur MacLeod's words were true.

Moushoom agreed as well, but he added that there was more that could be said about the matter. "Time will judge Louis Riel, Josephine, as it will judge all of us."

I believe that is so, but I cannot help but wonder what will be said about Monsieur Riel, and Batoche, and we Métis, in distant years to come. For now, though, my family is here around me and that is enough. As for promises, I vow that I will always hold my head high when I hear the name Métis. And I will always write the truth, no matter how hard it is to do that.

Epilogue

Josephine honoured those promises, although keeping the second one was not always easy. Recording the truth meant that the pages of her diary became a story of suffering.

Because Louis Riel had petitioned for their rights as well as those of the Métis, he had the support of many Native people. After the Resistance, a number of them were arrested, charged with murder, and tried. On November 27, 1885, eight of these men were publicly hanged at Fort Battleford. They were Kah-pay-pamah-chukwew (Wandering Spirit), Pah-pah-me-kee-sick (Walking the Sky), Manchoose (Bad Arrow), Kit-awah-ki-ni (Miserable Man), Nahpase (Iron Body), A-pis-chas-koos (Little Bear), Itka (Crooked Leg) and Way-wah-nitch (Man Without Blood). Singing death chants — Wandering Spirit sang a love song for his wife — they died bravely and with great dignity. It was the largest mass hanging in Canadian history, and would always remain so.

The small amount of money that Moushoom had in his tin box helped to hold off hunger for the Bouviers, but only just. As the weeks passed, many of their friends, relatives and neighbours left

Batoche. Others died of starvation, illness — even despair. Finally, in December, Michel took his family to Louise's sister in Prince Albert. It was hard to leave Adrian behind, but for the sake of their cabin and few remaining possessions, Michel's oldest son insisted on staying. Josephine found Christmas lonely without Adrian, but the visit cheered Louise and raised everyone's spirits.

A few months later, back in Batoche, Josephine's father and stepmother were granted land scrip for their farms, and just like that, a piece of paper declared that the land was theirs. Josephine sometimes wondered what life would have been like had the government done this when it should have, instead of delaying until the Métis felt they had no choice but to take action. The scrip was a good thing, but other matters had to be addressed. Although so much of what they had lost would be impossible to replace, Michel Bouvier and his wife applied to the government for compensation, as did their neighbours. Josephine's father calculated the value of the houses, buildings and livestock they had lost at $1800. But their application was denied, like that of so many others. After all, Michel and his wife had supported the rebels and he had fought against the government. They were on their own.

Now and again, they heard bits of news about their old friends. Some of it was bitterly sad. After the Battle of Batoche, Louis Riel's brother had arrived and taken Marguerite and the children back to St. Boniface. She passed away the spring after her husband's hanging, finally losing her battle with consumption. Marie-Angelique and Jean-Louis would remain with their paternal grandmother. His health fragile, One Arrow was released from prison, having served only a small part of his sentence. He died shortly after. Moushoom was deeply saddened, but he took comfort in what he was told were One Arrow's last words to the government: "Do not mis-treat my people." One Arrow had died as he had lived, a great chief of the Willow Cree.

Other news was happier. It seemed that Gabriel Dumont was still down in the United States, working for a man named Buffalo Bill Cody. Dumont was riding and shooting in Cody's Wild West Show. This made Moushoom laugh heartily. "What a thing! Gabriel working for a man named Buffalo," he said. "That Buffalo fellow had better watch out that Gabriel does not forget himself and think he is on a real hunt!"

Michel Bouvier began to make another fiddle, working slowly on the instrument in the evenings. Moushoom decided it was time to weave another *saencheur flechee,* and so he began, his arthritic fingers moving laboriously. Sometimes Josephine wondered if the two men were in silent competition to see who could make his project last longer. It was her father who completed his first, though. The house rang with music that night.

Josephine and Louise continued to work together keeping house in Moushoom's cabin. Moon died on a warm summer evening, and Moushoom buried him next to the other dogs. When Moushoom had a small stroke, Josephine took on his workload. She took great satisfaction in helping to rebuild the big house and outbuildings. Often she worked by Edmond's side, and as time passed their friendship deepened.

The Bouvier men never did forget the role the priests played during the battle for Batoche. Michel, though, softened enough to permit Armand to return to school when he was not needed to work at home. When he was old enough, Alexandre joined him.

It took four years of hard labour before the Bouviers felt they could breathe easily. As well as working the farm, Adrian, Armand and their father delivered firewood. Louise and Josephine collected and sold seneca root. One year, Adrian went out with some other men and gathered the buffalo bones that still lay out on the prairie. American factories bought the bones and made them into fertilizer and other items such as buttons and knife handles — a cart filled with close to half a ton of bones would bring in three dollars. The earnings let the family buy a few cows, a young bull and some chickens. Life was hard but good.

Moushoom finished his sash just after the sixth anniversary of the war. He died in his sleep a week later. As he had asked, he was buried near the river on Bouvier land, instead of in the cemetery, the sash wrapped around his waist. Michel Bouvier stood next to his father's grave and very slowly played "Whiskey Before Breakfast," which Moushoom had loved above all other Métis fiddle tunes.

The next day Edmond left, despite assurances that he was part of their family. Josephine did not try to change his decision. She understood enough of Edmond Swift Fox's nature to realize that with Moushoom's passing, it would be far too painful for him to remain at Batoche. He needed time alone to heal.

By 1891, Josephine had decided to attend the normal school in Regina and study to be a teacher. It had always been a dream of hers. But then her father was thrown from a horse and both of his legs were badly broken. It was not easy for Josephine to tame her restless spirit, but she abandoned her own plans. The family must come first, after all. She, Adrian and Armand worked the farm while Louise cared for their father. He recovered, but was never able to walk again without difficulty.

Although he never spoke of it, Michel Bouvier knew what his daughter had given up for his sake. Each year on January 1, he found the money to give her a new diary in Moushoom's memory. And on that day each year, with Louise's approval, Josephine read some of Anne Bouvier's diary aloud to her father and the rest of the family. Like her own diary, it was filled with wonderful stories.

Now and again Josephine and Emma exchanged letters. In time, though, the two friends drifted apart, as friends sometimes do. The letters grew less frequent and then stopped. The last news Josephine had of Emma MacLeod was a brief note and the newspaper clipping from the *Toronto Globe* of her wedding announcement. By this time, Adrian was courting a young Batoche woman. All he said was that he wished Emma happiness. Sometimes Josephine wondered if she herself would ever marry, but she did not wonder often. There was no time for romantic notions.

Not until July 24, 1900, did Josephine again see Edmond Swift Fox. It was during the St. Joseph's Day celebration, one that her father, Moïse Ouellette and others had been instrumental in beginning. What better way to honour the dead veterans than to celebrate in their names? Each year an ox was donated and slaughtered — Moïse had donated the first one — the ox representing the buffalo the

Métis had once hunted. This year the ox had been donated by Michel Bouvier.

Josephine was serving oxtail *rababoo* to hungry people. She looked up, and there Edmond was, right in front of her. He was older, but he was still Edmond.

"I had to come home," he told her. As Moushoom would say, Once a Sauvé from Batoche, always a Sauvé from Batoche. A few weeks later, Josephine wrote this in her diary:

Le 28 juillet 1900

How strange the year still looks. 1900. I wonder what Moushoom would think of it? I definitely know what he would think of the fact that I have said yes to Edmond Swift Fox, though. Josephine Bouvier Sauvé. I do like the look and sound of that.

Edmond and Josephine spent many happy years together as they raised a family of ten children: nine boys and a single girl. Edmond taught his wife to play billiards, and she taught him how to read. He always teased that he'd got the best part of that bargain, except when Josephine outplayed him at billiards, and it must be said that she did that often.

Her husband was a great consolation to her after Michel Bouvier and then Louise passed away. When

Armand and Adrian enlisted at the beginning of WWI to serve as snipers, it was Edmond who told her again and again that nothing would happen to either of them. Two Métis who had survived the Battle of Batoche were not destined to die in France. He was correct. Both men returned home to live out their lives with their wives and children.

In the summer of 1960, a story appeared in a national Canadian newspaper. Josephine and Edmond had been interviewed by their granddaughter, Michelle Bouvier Cameron, who worked for that paper.

The piece told the story of the Bouvier/Sauvé family and its role in what Michelle said had been "a resistance, not a rebellion, and perhaps even an invasion." She went on to describe her family, particularly her paternal grandparents, as veterans and heroes. Josephine and Edmond were very proud of their granddaughter, and often said that Moushoom must be as well.

A few weeks later, Josephine received a package from Newfoundland. Edmond commented that it was a strange thing, because they did not know anyone out there.

When Josephine opened the package, it contained a letter as well as a small object wrapped in tissue paper. This is what she read aloud to Edmond.

Dear Mrs. Sauvé,

It was with real interest that I read a newspaper article about you and your husband some time ago. History has always been a passion of mine, and so the piece caught my attention. It described you as veterans, which is a coincidence, since my great-grandfather was also a veteran. He was Corporal James Coates, who served in The Royal Canadian Regiment. He fought at Batoche in 1885. Like many soldiers, he brought back souvenirs, and although most are gone, one has been passed down through the years. It eventually came to me. I have always treasured it.

My great-grandfather was proud of his military service. I am proud of him as well. They tell me he used to say that we cannot rewrite history or change the past. All we can do is make new things happen. Good things.

This is yours, Mrs. Sauvé.

Sincerely,
Mrs. Margaret Coates

In the tissue paper was Anne Bouvier's pocket watch, which was once again running. The watch was buried with Josephine when she died several months later. She and Edmond rest at Batoche in the St. Antoine Cemetery.

Historical Note

Traditional Métis Life

When you see or hear the name Métis, a number of things probably come to mind. One might be the Red River cart, which the Métis developed for use in the buffalo hunts. Constructed of wood and fastened together with leather, its enormous wheels made it possible to travel over marshy or muddy conditions while carrying heavy loads. The carts floated, and were easily repaired. A single cart made a good deal of noise, as the wooden parts ground against each other. A train of dozens of carts could be heard for kilometres.

There is the Métis sash, the three-metre-long wool *ceinture fléchée* (in the Michif language, *saencheur flechee*). At one time these sashes were finger woven, a technique that did not require a loom. It was often possible to tell where someone was from by the colours and design of his or her sash. Later on, sashes were purchased or acquired as a trade item. A *ceinture fléchée* was worn as a ceremonial piece of clothing, but it could also be used as a rope or a scarf.

Then there is Métis fiddle music. It is quite different from Canadian or Scottish fiddling. The style is bouncier, and sounds as though the fiddler is accompanying herself or himself. This was necessary in the days when a single fiddle might be the only instrument available. Fiddle tunes varied from community to community, as bars were added or changed.

The Métis way of life was distinctive. Strip farms were a necessity to Métis people, just as they had been for the first French settlers in Quebec. These long narrow river-lot farms gave people access to water as well as a means of transportation. To have no direct access to the Saskatchewan River would have been unthinkable.

The Métis had their own language. It was called Michif, and like the word Métis it means "mixed." It was a combination of French and Native language, depending on the community. Josephine's diary would have been written in the French her mother taught her, but she and the other Métis characters would have spoken Michif. In their community of Batoche, the mixture used French nouns and Cree verbs. *"Li fournoo kishitayw,"* Michif for "The oven is hot," uses the French for "furnace" or "oven," and the Cree for "is hot." A girl such as Josephine would have made up her own spelling for her diary entries, based on the way the words were pronounced.

When a Métis told a story, it was very important to acknowledge the story's source. That is why Moushoom takes such pains to explain where some of his stories originate, even when it means going back through generations of storytellers. The Michif language nearly disappeared after the grim years following the Battle of Batoche. It was a time of great prejudice against the Métis, as well as a time of enormous suffering.

Today much has changed. Many Métis associations exist to support the rights of the people. There are Michif language programs, books and CDs. In the Rossignol Community Schools at Île-à-la-Crosse, Saskatchewan, Michif is part of the curriculum. In spite of this, the possibility that Michif will be extinct by 2050 is a real one.

The Métis considered themselves to be a new nation, and it was into this proud and independent nation that Louis Riel was born on October 22, 1844. He came into the world at his maternal grandparents' farm, which stood at the forks of the Red and Seine Rivers, near St. Boniface. His father, Louis Riel senior, and his mother, Julie Lagimodière, eventually built their own house on the east side of the Red River.

Riel's childhood was probably much like that of the fictional Bouvier children. Like them, he spent a great deal of time with his grandparents. His grandmother, Marie-Anne Gaboury, had been one of the first white women to come out to the Northwest. Her husband, Jean-Baptiste Lagimodière, had been a trader and a voyageur. If they told him stories, young Louis would have heard about their many adventures, of how they had once been captured by Sarcee warriors, of how they had escaped and raced for their lives across the prairie. One year, his grandmother had even borne a child right out on the open prairie, although unlike Moushoom's wife, she had only her husband to help her.

The character Josephine was raised to be intensely proud of her Métis heritage. So was Riel, who had one-eighth Native blood, his paternal grandmother having been a French–Chipewyan Métis. Riel's Catholic family was very religious, and education was highly valued. At first he attended a school run by the Grey Nuns, and then moved on to a school operated by the Christian Brothers. It was here, at the age of fourteen, that Louis was noticed by Bishop Taché. The bishop saw that young Riel had the qualities of a scholar, and more importantly, the makings of a Métis priest. With his parents' blessings, the bishop arranged for Riel to study in Canada at the Petit Séminaire de Montréal.

Studying for the priesthood did not suit Riel. When in 1864 he learned that his father had died, he left the school the next year. He tried working as a law clerk to help support his family. Finally, after spending time in the United States, Riel decided to return to Red River in 1868.

The Red River Resistance

This novel refers to two important events in Métis history. The first is the Red River Resistance of

1869. The second is the Northwest Resistance of 1885. They used to be more commonly referred to as the Red River and the Northwest Rebellions. Louis Riel took the role of leader in both of them, as the Métis people struggled for their rights.

The Red River settlement, which was part of a large area called Rupert's Land, had long been administered by the Hudson's Bay Company. By 1869 there were approximately 5,700 Métis, 4,100 English-speaking people of mixed blood, 1,500 Canadians and 550 First Nations people at Red River. Tensions and conflicts over trading privileges had always existed, but when the HBC sold Rupert's Land to Canada that year, an uneasy situation arose. The government began to survey land already occupied by Métis families. Instead of keeping the original strip farms stretching up from the river, the surveyors sectioned the land in squares, the very squares that so disturbed Moushoom in this novel. In October of 1869, Louis Riel and sixteen Métis stopped a crew of surveyors on Métis land. The Red River Resistance had begun. Riel and his followers formed the National Committee of Métis to protect their land interests. They captured Fort Garry and set up a provisional government. When the new Lieutenant-Governor, William McDougall, arrived from Canada, he was sent away. The Métis intended to govern themselves.

An Ontario man named Thomas Scott, who had been working in the area, was the driving force behind a band of Canadians heading for Fort Garry in January 1870. Scott, who was fiercely anti-French and anti-Catholic, wanted only English-speaking whites to settle the prairies. He had collected around himself a group of men who shared his ideas.

The Métis arrested and jailed them. At the end of that month, Prime Minister John A. Macdonald sent Donald Smith, a government messenger, to the Red River settlement. He was to explain the government's policy to the Métis. Frustrated and disheartened with the fact that they were still being ignored, Riel and the provisional government sent him back to Ottawa with a Métis Bill of Rights.

Thomas Scott became a difficult prisoner, and hostile to everything for which the Métis stood. Riel ordered him tried. Scott was sentenced to death and executed on March 4, 1869. The execution, which went very badly, is the event that haunts Michel Bouvier in this story. The firing squad fired, but only three bullets hit Scott, none of them killing him. It was left to one of the men to put a revolver to Scott's head, and pull the trigger. What was considered a lawful execution by the Métis people, was seen as murder by those in Upper Canada.

When the Red River settlement entered Confederation in 1870 as Manitoba — the reason Riel is called the father of Manitoba — many people in English Canada remained enraged by Thomas Scott's death. Riel had no choice but to accept a five-year voluntary exile to the United States, where he lived in both Minnesota and North Dakota.

During the time he was in exile, Riel was elected to Canadian Parliament three times. Edward Blake, the Premier of Ontario, placed a $5000 bounty on Riel's head, a bounty intended to keep him from taking his seat. Fearing for his life, and under the threat of that bounty, the courage it took for Riel to come into Canada, slip into the Parliament Buildings and sign the register there is difficult to imagine. He was often depressed, and spent periods of time in asylums — what today we call psychiatric hospitals. To the very end, he insisted that he had not been mentally ill.

By 1878 Riel was back in the Montana Territory. It was there that he met a young Métis woman named Marguerite Monet dit Bellehumeur. They wed *à la façon du pays* on April 28, 1881; the next year, they were married by a priest. At one point, Riel was working on a sheep ranch owned by a man named Henry Macdonald. Marguerite took care of the owners' baby. She cooked for the ranch hands, and spent hours beading moccasins and bags. She also crocheted, and made a pair of wristlets using white and blue yarn for the Macdonald baby. Those wristlets are in the collection of the Montana Historical Society, and were the inspiration for the gift Marguerite sends to Louise.

The Northwest Resistance

When Louis Riel arrived at Batoche in July of 1884, having been persuaded to come by Gabriel Dumont and three other Métis representatives, James Isbister, Michel Dumont and Moïse Ouellette, he had not only brought his wife and two children with him. He also carried the legacy of the Red River Resistance. Prime Minister John A. Macdonald had not forgotten the events of 1869–1870. Although not all historians agree, some are of the opinion that as the months went on, Macdonald purposely aggravated the situation in the Northwest. Louis Riel had few options in a situation where the government would not recognize the rights of the Métis. Under his leadership a Provisional Council was formed. Riel called it the Exovedate, which was the word that Josephine and many others could not pronounce. It meant "those who have left the flock."

On March 17, the rumour reached Batoche that more than 500 mounted police were on their way to arrest Riel. The Métis reacted by raiding the Kerr brothers' store, and taking prisoners. Riel formed his Provisional Government the next day, and Dumont took charge of the military. On March 25, Dumont and his Métis soldiers fought a force of North-West Mounted Police and volunteers commanded by Superintendent Leif Newry Fitzroy Crozier. The Métis would have destroyed them, had Riel not given the order to cease fire.

There was no involvement on the part of the Métis in the killings at Frog Lake, and yet the public still blamed Riel. Macdonald decided the time was right to put the Métis in their place, and so called in Major-General Frederick Dobson Middleton to do the job. Major-General Thomas Bland Strange was ordered to march from Calgary and engage Big Bear and his warriors. He was then to join Middleton. Lieutenant-Colonel William Dillon Otter and his men would reinforce Fort Battleford.

Although Riel had sought the support of the First Nations, only some gave it. Josephine would have been aware of only some of the facts of their participation. Big Bear's war chief, Wandering Spirit, led the attack on Fish Creek. Both men paid the price for their insurrection. Wandering Spirit was hanged, and Big Bear was sentenced to three years in Stony Mountain Penitentiary, although he served only two of them. By the time he was released, though, he was a broken and sick man.

Other First Nations leaders suffered similar fates. Camped at a spot called Cut Knife Creek, Cree chief Poundmaker's village was attacked by Colonel Otter's forces on May 2. The Cree, led by Poundmaker's war chief Fine Day, were outnumbered, but they still defeated their enemy. Poundmaker urged his warriors not to continue their actions against the soldiers, but he was unsuccessful. He was tried, found guilty, and sentenced to three years in Stony Mountain. He served only one of those years, but that was enough to ruin his health. Poundmaker died four months after his release.

One Arrow's trial was carried on through an interpreter whose words continually left the chief confused. According to the Crown, One Arrow had associated with the Métis at Batoche, and so had broken his treaty with the Queen. On this basis, One Arrow was blamed, tried and sentenced within six minutes.

Equally unfair was the treatment of the First Nations men who had been arrested and charged with murder for their activities at Frog Lake. Lieutenant-Governor Edgar Dewdney decided to make the executions a public event. The prime minister agreed. Macdonald would write to him saying: *The execution of Riel and of the Indians will, I hope, have a good effect on the Métis and convince the Red Man that the White Man governs.*

When Chief One Arrow died on April 25, 1886, soon after being released from prison, he was buried in the St. Boniface Cemetery, beside Louis Riel's gravesite. His body remained there for 120 years, far from his people and his home. In 2007 the people of The One Arrow First Nation asked that Chief One Arrow's remains be returned to them. Their request was granted. His old gravestone was left behind at St. Boniface, but the chief's body was brought back to the reserve. After a four-day traditional wake and a funeral service, Chief One Arrow was buried there on August 28, 2007.

When General Middleton's troops entered Métis land, what resulted was the Resistance of 1885. Scholars have long referred to the Resistance as a rebellion, but in the eyes of the Métis, no rebellion was involved. The people of Batoche were simply resisting the efforts of the Canadian government to invade and rule their land. Though this term has been much debated, it remains the position of the Métis today.

In the end, Louis Riel was charged with high treason on June 6, 1885. If he had been tried in Manitoba, he would probably have faced a jury of sympathetic Métis. But the trial was held in Regina. The jury was made up of English Protestants, and the judge had close ties to the Canadian government. Riel's lawyers were forbidden by the judge to refer to the events that had led up to the actions for which he was being tried, and Riel was only allowed to speak in his own defence at the very end of the trial.

His words were wasted. He had pled not guilty, certain that the law would be with him, but he was wrong. The jury found him guilty. They recommended mercy, but he was sentenced to hang on September 18, and although his execution was delayed by a series of appeals, they were unsuccessful.

Louis Riel's Execution and its Aftermath

Many people, particularly in Quebec, thought the sentence was unfair. The fact was that John A. Macdonald had said that Riel "shall hang, though every dog in Quebec shall bark in his favour." Louis Riel was executed on November 16, 1885. His remains were returned to his wife, and he was buried at St. Boniface.

Louis Riel's friends and family were now left without his powerful influence. His wife Marguerite died of pneumonia after a long battle with the coughing sickness — what we now call tuberculosis — at St. Boniface in May of 1886. She was buried next to her husband. Marie-Angelique died of diphtheria in 1878. Her brother Jean-Louis died in 1908 of complications resulting from a buggy accident. Louis Riel has no direct descendants.

Riel's lieutenant, Gabriel Dumont, remained in the United States, where he performed as a skilled marksman in Buffalo Bill Cody's Wild West Show for a few years. When amnesty was granted to the

Resistance participants, he returned to Canada in 1888, and then to Batoche in 1893. Dumont passed away on May 19, 1906, and was buried in the Batoche cemetery near the other veterans.

Marie-Antoinette, the St. Antoine church bell, was taken back to Millbrook, Ontario, by three soldiers, Private Jack Stainthorpe, Private Ira Nattrass and Sergeant Ed McCorry. For several decades it hung in the town firehall. It was then put on display in the local Royal Canadian Legion #402. Over the years, Métis leaders asked that the bell be returned to Batoche, but the answer was always no. In 1991 the bell was stolen from the Legion, as were Sergeant McCorry's medals. At the time of this printing, the bell is still missing.

Other treasures, though, have found their way home. Gabriel Dumont's billiard table was probably confiscated by Colonel Samuel L. Bedson, a transport officer in the Canadian forces. Bedson was also a prison warden. It is likely that he took the table back to Stony Mountain Penitentiary near Winnipeg, the same prison in which One Arrow, Big Bear, Poundmaker and the convicted Métis served their sentences. Later on, the billiard table was kept at the warden's home. After many decades, it was given to Parks Canada, where it sat in a warehouse. It was returned to the Batoche National Historic Site in 2006. The table needed new felt, and it had received nicks and scratches over the years, but it was in good condition.

Louis Riel's Legacy

Although Riel's life was honoured by Métis people in many ways over the years, on February 18, 2008, the first annual Louis Riel Day was celebrated in Manitoba. That in itself is a special event, but what had been returned to the Métis people is even more remarkable. After the Battle of Batoche, Riel and two unnamed companions fled to the settlement of Halcro, about 45 kilometres from Batoche. There they were taken in by a Métis woman named Margaret Halcro, who hid them in her root cellar. Three days later, Louis Riel decided to give himself up. He gave Margaret Halcro his HBC presentation sash in gratitude for what she had done, and then he and his companions surrendered to Big Tom Hourie and two other scouts about 300 metres from Margaret's home.

The sash, which over the years had simply been kept in drawer or a trunk, was passed down through Margaret Halcro's family along with the story. In 2008 her descendent, seventy-six-year-old Marian Hackworth of Dawson Creek, B.C., contacted the province's Northeast Métis Association, telling its president that she had the sash. It was authenticated, returned to the Manitoba Métis Federation, and is now on display at the St. Boniface Museum.

Today Batoche is a national historic site. It is more than that, though; for the Métis, it is hallowed land. Each July since 1970, people have come to Batoche to celebrate Métis culture through the Back to Batoche Days festival. Everyone is welcome. They camp in tents, trailers, even tipis. Some compete in voyageur games, throwing hatchets or carrying heavy loads. There is a bannock-baking contest. Visitors can sample traditional food, listen to storytellers or purchase traditional crafts. There is jigging, square dancing and fiddling. And on Sunday, people gather at the cemetery where a Mass is said, and the struggle that took place there is remembered. So are the people who were a part of that struggle.

Riel's death outraged Francophones, driving a wedge between them and English Canada that continues to this day. For many years, Riel and his cause have been the topic of controversy and discussion. He was, after all, a man as complex as the patterns in a *ceinture fléchée.* Some have viewed him as a visionary, a person who could see a future of harmony and peace between the Métis and their neighbours. He has been regarded as a martyr, as someone who was unfairly executed. Others considered him a traitor. The Métis people, though, have never had any doubt about Louis Riel. For them, and for many other Canadians, he remains a hero.

Louis Riel in 1878, after fighting for Métis rights during the 1870 Resistance. His wife Marguerite died of pneumonia following years of suffering from tuberculosis, in 1886.

Riel's children, Jean-Louis and Marie-Angelique. Marie-Angelique died of diphtheria in 1878. Jean-Louis died in 1908 after a buggy accident.

After the 1870 Resistance, many Métis moved from Manitoba to Saskatchewan, in hope of a better life.

Métis fiddle music has a sound all its own. The "Red River Jig" is uniquely Métis.

When the buffalo roamed the plains, the buffalo hunt was a yearly event for the Métis and for many First Nations people.

Gabriel Dumont, one of the Métis' most experienced buffalo hunters, rode to Montana to ask Louis Riel to help the Saskatchewan Métis gain title to their land.

Cree traders during negotiations at Fort Pitt. Some of the First Nations bands sided with Riel, Dumont and the Métis. Others did not wish to fight.

The Métis forces met those of General Middleton for the first time at the Battle of Fish Creek.

THE GATLING GUN.

The Gatling gun consists of a number of breach-loading rifled barrels revolving about a central shaft. These barrels are loaded and fired while revolving, and after each discharge the empty cartridge shells fall out. Each barrel is fired only once in a revolution of the gun, so that with each single revolution of the gun ten shots are fired, while the gun can revolve twice a second if need be. This would give a fire of 1,200 shots per minute. The feeding of the gun is simple. A long tin box, called a feed case, holding a row of cartridges, is held by one man perpendicularly over a hopper at the breach of the gun, and cartridges fall in as they are wanted. Another man turns the crank by which the gun is revolved, and the firing goes on continuously.

General Middleton's soldiers used a Gatling gun to fire high-velocity bullets at the Métis fighters. The Gatling gun's firepower was too much for even the Métis crack shots.

The Battle of Batoche begins.

Major-General Middleton's soldiers were ordered to quell the Métis uprising in the Batoche area, after the telegraph lines at Clark's Crossing were cut.

This sketch of the steamship *Northcote,* under fire from Métis fighters, appeared in the *Illustrated War News* on May 9, 1885.

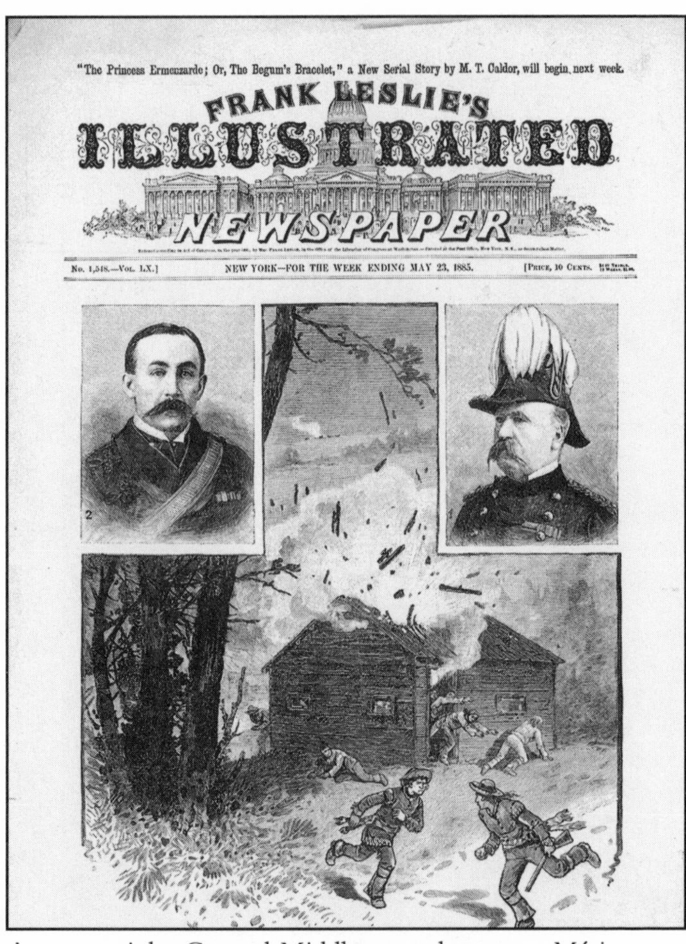
"The Princess Ermenzarde; Or, The Begum's Bracelet," a New Serial Story by M. T. Caldor, will begin next week.

FRANK LESLIE'S ILLUSTRATED NEWSPAPER

No. 1,548.—Vol. LX.] NEW YORK—FOR THE WEEK ENDING MAY 23, 1885. [Price, 10 Cents.

At upper right, General Middleton; at bottom, a Métis home being hit by shells. Most of the homes in and around Batoche were burned by the army.

Soldiers advance on dug-in Métis fighters.

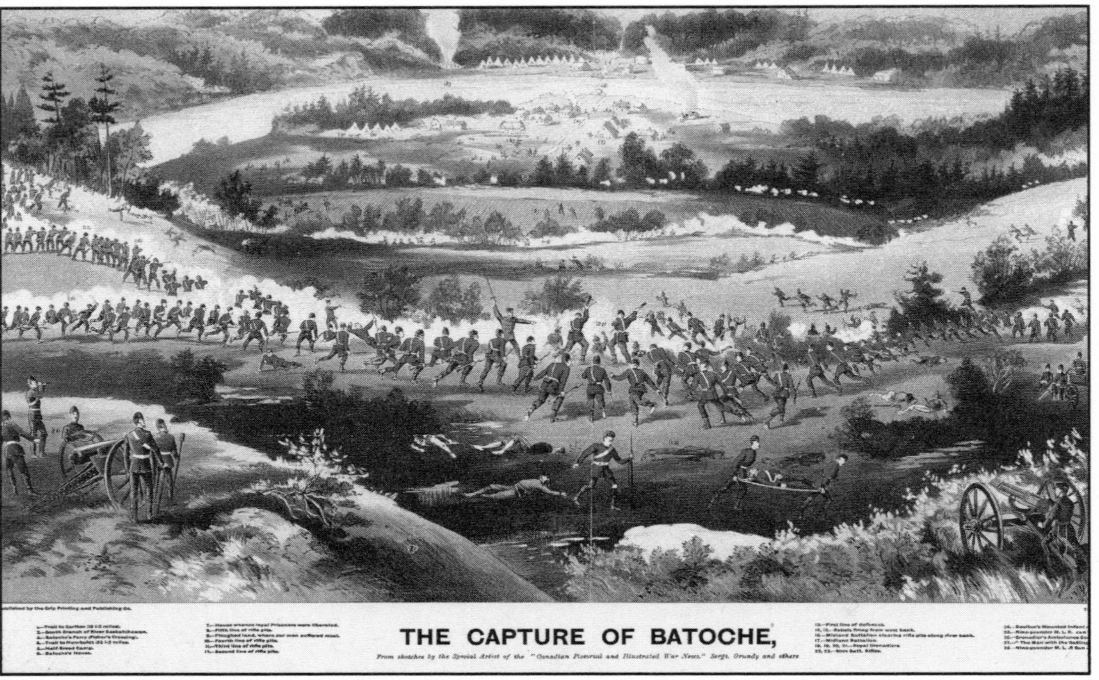

After three days of fighting, Middleton's forces finally captured Batoche.

Cree Chief Poundmaker was imprisoned after the Resistance. He died soon after being released from Stony Mountain Prison.

Nine of the Métis who fought and died in the Resistance are buried in a mass grave in the cemetery at Batoche.

Michif Glossary

Abain: interjection, such as "I'll be darned"
bābee: baby
Batochien: insult meaning Batoche dog/cur
bell anzhelik: rat root
belmyr: stepmother
bengs: pieces of sweet fried dough
li Blawn: the whites
Le Boon Jeu: Jesus
boulets: venison and muskrat (or other meat) and vegetables, all rolled together into small meatballs
chirāān: Northern lights
dilet kwyee: sour milk
galet: bannock
gárso: boy
googoosh: boogeyman
grawdpayrs: long flat dumplings boiled in chicken broth
Kanayaen: French-Canadian (female)
Kanayah: French-Canadian (male)
Laenjee Graw: Mardi Gras
Mafway jeu: exclamation, such as "oh my god"
mársee: thank you
ma nohkom: my grandmother
mo nook: my uncle
Pimbahtaw: Run or Go (order to sled dogs)
rababoo: stew made of vegetables and meat
roogaroo: werewolf
saencheur flechee: colourful sash worn by Métis people

Michif Glossary (continued)

soup di pwaw: pea soup
tart de vyawnd: meat pie made of venison and pork
ma tawnt: my aunt
turtulage: beating out a rhythm with spoons
Vawndarzee Saen: Good Friday
vylōōn: fiddle
zhounn: yellow
Zhour di Lāh: New Year's Day
Zhour di Pawk: Easter
Zhour di Rwāy: holy feast day of the Three Kings
Zhour di Sawndr: Ash Wednesday

Cree Glossary

kinikinik: mixture of red willow bark and bearberry leaves
Ma-ma-kwa-se-sak: the little people who live in the caves
masinahican: book
mihkwânikwacâs: red squirrel
nichimoose: sweetheart
Otipemisiwak: they are free; they have no owners; the ones who own themselves; the independent ones
shaganappi: braided buffalo hide used as harness or rope

French Glossary

à la façon du pays: marriage in the custom of the country

bal à l'huile: dance held by lamplight

bonhomme jigueur: jigger

capot: long coat

cariole: dogsled

la danse du crochet: hook dance, also called "Drops of Brandy" or "Strip the Willow" for the songs that often accompany it

éclipse: eclipse

flèche: arrow

Mardi gras: Fat Tuesday, the day before Lent

médaille miraculeuse: a medal that honours the immaculate conception of the Virgin Mary

parfleche: leather packet

le petit provisoire: provisional council created during the Resistance of 1885

piquette: homebrew

rameaux: palm fronds given out on Palm Sunday

septième: seventh daughter; one with the power of healing

tapis: small wool blanket with bells, worn by a sled dog

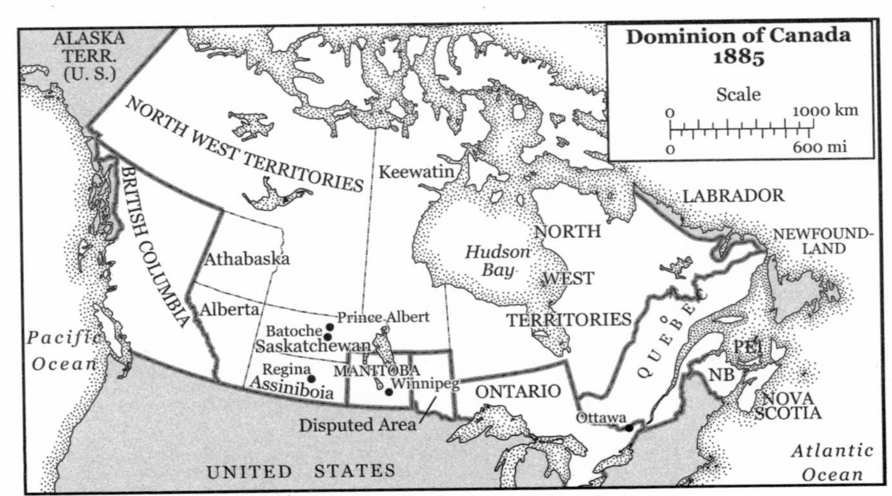

Canada in 1885. The Canadian Pacific Railroad was completed late that year.

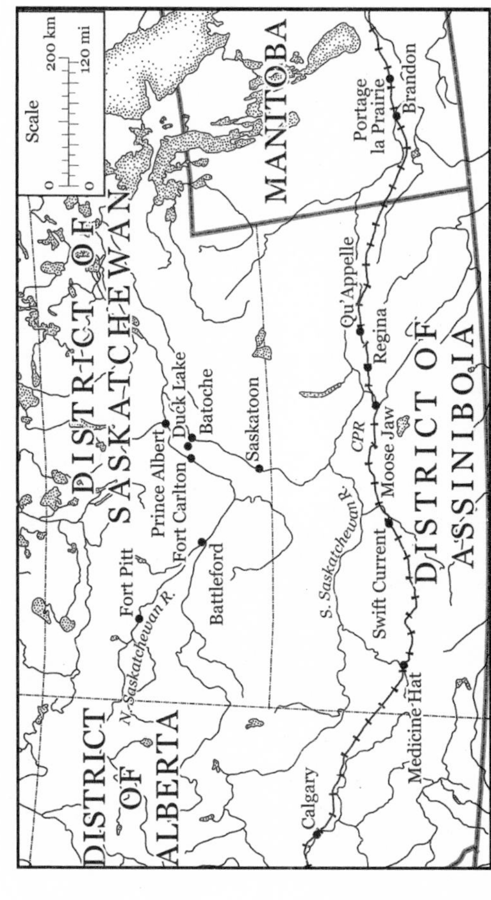

The area involved in the 1885 Northwest Resistance.

Acknowledgments

Cover cameo: (Detail from) *Bernadita* by Robert Henri (Cozaddale, Ohio, June 24, 1865 — July 12, 1929, New York, New York); oil on canvas, October 1922; 24 1/8 in. x 20 1/8 in. (61.28 cm x 51.12 cm); gift of the San Diego Wednesday Club; courtesy of San Diego Museum of Art 1926:138

Cover background: (Detail, lightened, from) *The Capture of Batoche,* Library and Archives Canada C-001728, MIKAN number 2837525; also used in full on page 218

Page 204 upper: *Louis Riel,* Glenbow Museum NA-504-3

Page 204 lower: *Marguerite Riel,* Saskatchewan Archives Board Identifier: R-D2169

Page 205: *Jean-Louis and Angelique Riel,* Library and Archives Canada PA-139072

Page 206: *Metis children and Red River cart, Pembina area, Manitoba,* Glenbow Museum NA-1406-30

Page 207: *Metis dance, Pembina, Manitoba,* Glenbow Museum NA-1406-23

Page 208: *Buffalo hunt, Red River,* Glenbow Museum NA-1406-7

Page 209: *Gabriel Dumont, Red River, Alberta,* Glenbow Museum NA-1063-1

Page 210: *Cree men and traders at Fort Pitt, Saskatchewan,* Glenbow Museum NA-1323-4

Page 211: *The battle of Fish Creek, April 2, [1885],* Library and Archives Canada C-001728

Page 212: *Gatling gun used in Riel Rebellion,* Glenbow Museum NA-1032-3

Page 213: *Start of the battle of Batoche, Saskatchewan,* Glenbow Museum NA-363-38

Page 214: *Major-General Middleton,* Saskatchewan Archives Board Identifier: R-A5524

Page 215: *Steamboat "Northcote" under fire during the Riel Rebellion,* Glenbow Museum NA-1353-11
Page 216: *Canada – Fighting in the North West [1885],* Library and Archives Canada C-097664
Page 217: C.W. Jefferys, *Battle of Batoche, 1885,* Library and Archives Canada C-073636
Page 219: *Portrait of Poundmaker, Cree Chief, at Stony Mountain Penitentiary* Glenbow Museum NA-292-3
Page 220: *Batoche Cemetery (01),* Saskatchewan Archives Board Identifier: R-B5405-5 (55-300-22)

Newspaper clippings from PaperofRecord.com: pages 20 and 41 *Winnipeg Daily Times* January 8, 1885; page 58 *Qu'Appelle Vidette;* page 110–111 *The Toronto World* March 12, 1885; pages 131–132 *The Toronto World* March 24, 1885; page 137 *Winnipeg Daily Times* March 26, 1885; page 154 *Winnipeg Daily Times* April 18, 1885.

Pages 224 and 225: Maps by Paul Heersink/Paperglyphs. Map data © 2000 Government of Canada with permission from Natural Resources Canada.

Thanks to Barbara Hehner for her careful checking of the manuscript, to Lawrence Barkwell of the Louis Riel Institute and author of *Metis Legacy Vol. I , Metis Legacy Vol. II, La Lawng: Michif Peekishkwewin, Vols. I & II, Batoche 1885: The Militia of the Metis Liberation Movement* and *Women of the 1885 Resistance,* for lending his expertise re Louis Riel and the Resistance. Our thanks also to Tyrone Tootoosis for checking the Cree glossary; Bruce Flamont, one of the last remaining Michif speakers, for checking the Michif terms and glossary and commenting on the manuscript; and Martine Faubert for checking the French words and glossary. Our thanks also to Dr. Bill Waiser, author of *Saskatchewan: A New History* and other historical books, for his helpful input.

For Bill and Kelly

About the Author

Maxine Trottier's roots reach back to New France, where in the seventeenth century two of her ancestors were *filles du roi* (something she discovered while researching her book *Alone in an Untamed Land)*. Later generations would become founding families of Fort Pontchartraim du Détroit under the command of Antoine Laumet de La Mothe, sieur de Cadillac. It was near Detroit that her ancestor Pierre Roy wed a native woman of the Miami tribe, Marguerite Ouebankikoue; their family and descendents remained in the area and flourished.

Maxine's Métis ancestors fought at Fort Detroit during the War of 1812. Three of her "uncles"— Alexis, Pierre, and Julien Labute, the grandsons of Pierre Roy — were each captains of battalions in the 2nd Regiment of the Essex Militia at that time.

In 1803, her Métis ancestor Georges Drouillard was recruited for an American expedition, one that would cross the entire continent. Over the next three years, Drouillard acted as an interpreter and hunter for Meriwether Lewis and William Clark — the famous Lewis and Clark Expedition. Guided by the Shoshone woman Sacagawea, the expedition travelled more than 13,000 kilometres from St.

Charles, Missouri, to the Pacific Ocean and back again. Drouillard's ability to communicate with First Nations people using hand signs had been invaluable during the journey.

Maxine is very familiar with some of the food described in this book, since her grandmother, Mary LaBute, prepared it. Fried muskrat, *grandpères, begns* and *galet* were often part of meals at her grandparents' home. So were sturgeon and home-made sturgeon caviar from fish that her grandfather would catch himself.

Her grandfather, Mark LaBute, played the fiddle, one that he made himself as a young man. The sounds of "Big John MacNeil," "The Red River Jig" and other tunes, always accompanied by *turtualge,* would ring out at house parties.

Maxine has written a picture book about Louis Riel, *Storm at Batoche.* Her first book in the Dear Canada series, *Alone in an Untamed Land,* was a nominee for the Silver Birch and Hackmatack awards, and was named an OLA Best Book. Her second Dear Canada, *The Death of My Country,* was an Honour Book for the Geoffrey Bilson Award for Historical Fiction. Both books are available in French (*Seule au Nouveau Monde* and *Mon Pays à Feu et à Sang).*

Maxine is the author of *Terry Fox, A Story of Hope;* she donated all royalties for that book to the

Terry Fox Foundation. She has also written other picture books, such as *Laura: A Childhood Tale of Laura Secord* and the Mr. Christie's Award Winner *Claire's Gift,* as well as the Scholastic Canada Biographies series for younger readers. She won the CLA Book of the Year Award for *The Tiny Kite of Eddie Wing,* and was nominated for it for *A Circle of Silver,* her first novel.

Over the years, Maxine has been an avid historical re-enactor, spending many weeks at forts and historical sites across Canada, from Fortress Louisbourg in Nova Scotia to crewing on a tall ship (a replica of the HMS *Tecumseh*) on the Great Lakes. She currently resides in Newfoundland, overlooking Bonavista Bay, with its amazing sights of surfacing whales and looming icebergs.

The text has been printed on chlorine-free paper
made with 30% post-consumer waste.

While the events described and some of the characters in this book may be based on actual historical events and real people, Josephine Bouvier is a fictional character created by the author, and her diary is a work of fiction.

National Library of Canada Cataloguing in Publication

Trottier, Maxine
Blood upon our land : the North West Resistance diary of Josephine Bouvier / Maxine Trottier.

(Dear Canada)
ISBN 978-0-545-99905-2

1. Riel, Louis, 1844-1885--Juvenile fiction. 2. Riel Rebellion, 1885--Juvenile fiction. I. Title. II. Series.
PS8589.R685B56 2009 jC813'.54 C2008-905170-X

ISBN 10 978-0-545-99905-7

6 5 4 3 2 1 Printed in Canada 09 10 11 12 13

The display type was set in Minion.
The text was set in Bembo.

First printing January 2009

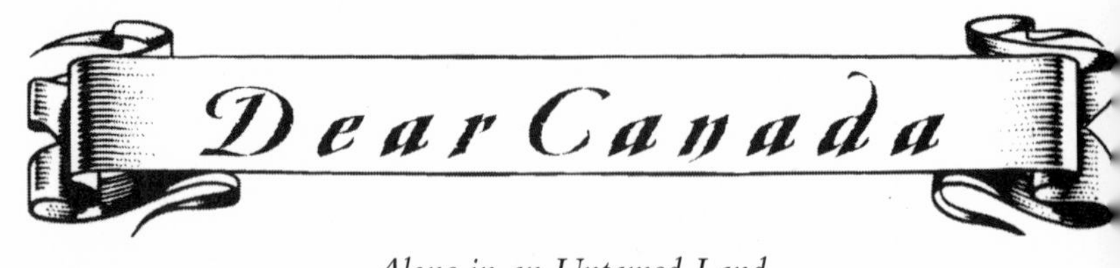

Alone in an Untamed Land
The Filles du Roi *Diary of Hélène St. Onge*
by Maxine Trottier

Banished from Our Home
The Acadian Diary of Angélique Richard
by Sharon Stewart

Brothers Far from Home
The World War I Diary of Eliza Bates
by Jean Little

Days of Toil and Tears
The Child Labour Diary of Flora Rutherford
by Sarah Ellis

The Death of My Country
The Plains of Abraham Diary of Geneviève Aubuchon
by Maxine Trottier

Footsteps in the Snow
The Red River Diary of Isobel Scott
by Carol Matas

If I Die Before I Wake
The Flu Epidemic Diary of Fiona Macgregor
by Jean Little

No Safe Harbour
The Halifax Explosion Diary of Charlotte Blackburn
by Julie Lawson

Not a Nickel to Spare
The Great Depression Diary of Sally Cohen
by Perry Nodelman

An Ocean Apart
The Gold Mountain Diary of Chin Mei-ling
by Gillian Chan

Orphan at My Door
The Home Child Diary of Victoria Cope
by Jean Little

A Prairie as Wide as the Sea
The Immigrant Diary of Ivy Weatherall
by Sarah Ellis

Prisoners in the Promised Land
The Ukrainian Internment Diary of Anya Soloniuk
by Marsha Skrypuch

A Rebel's Daughter
The 1837 Rebellion Diary of Arabella Stevenson
by Janet Lunn

A Ribbon of Shining Steel
The Railway Diary of Kate Cameron
by Julie Lawson

A Season for Miracles
Twelve Tales of Christmas

A Trail of Broken Dreams
The Gold Rush Diary of Harriet Palmer
by Barbara Haworth-Attard

Turned Away
The World War II Diary of Devorah Bernstein
by Carol Matas

Where the River Takes Me
The Hudson's Bay Company Diary of Jenna Sinclair
by Julie Lawson

Whispers of War
The War of 1812 Diary of Susanna Merritt
by Kit Pearson

Winter of Peril
The Newfoundland Diary of Sophie Loveridge
by Jan Andrews

With Nothing But Our Courage
The Loyalist Diary of Mary MacDonald
by Karleen Bradford

Go to www.scholastic.ca/dearcanada for information on the Dear Canada Series — see inside the books, read an excerpt or a review, post a review, and more.